ANGEL, ESQUIRE

Edgar Wallace wrote this novel and three short stories featuring Angel, Esquire: "The Yellow Box"; "The Silver Charm," and "A Case for Angel Esquire." We include them after the novel.

ORISON SWETT MARDEN

2015 by McAllister Editions (MCALLISTEREDITIONS@GMAIL.COM). This book is a classic, and a product of its time. It does not reflect the same views on race, gender, sexuality, ethnicity, and interpersonal relations as it would if it was written today.

CONTENTS

I. — THE LOMBARD STREET DEPOSIT

MR. WILLIAM SPEDDING, of the firm of Spedding, Mortimer and Larach, Solicitors, bought the site in Lombard Street in the conventional way. The property came into the market on the death of an old lady who lived at Market Harborough, who has nothing to do with this story, and it was put up to auction in the orthodox fashion. Mr. William Spedding secured the site at 106,000, a sum sufficiently large to excite the interest of all the evening papers and a great number of the morning journals as well. As a matter of exact detail, I may add that plans were produced and approved by the city surveyor for the erection of a building of a peculiar type. The city surveyor was a little puzzled by the interior arrangement of the new edifice, but as it fulfilled all the requirements of the regulations governing buildings in the City of London, and no fault could be found either with the external appearance—its facade had been so artfully designed that you might pass a dozen times a day without the thought occurring that this new building was anything out of the common ruck—and as the systems of ventilation and light were beyond reproach, he passed the plans with a shrug of his shoulders.

"I cannot understand, Mr. Spedding," he said, laying his forefinger on the blue print, "how your client intends securing privacy. There is a lobby and one big hall. Where are the private offices, and what is the idea of this huge safe in the middle of the hall, and where are the clerks to sit? I suppose he will have clerks? Why, man, he won't have a minute's peace!"

Mr. Spedding smiled grimly. "He will have all the peace he wants," he said. "And the vaults—I should have thought that vaults would be the very thing you wanted for this." He tapped the corner of the sheet where was inscribed decorously: "Plan for the erection of a New Safe Deposit."

"There is the safe," said Mr. Spedding, and smiled again.

This William Spedding, now unhappily no longer with us—he died suddenly, as I will relate—was a large, smooth man with a suave manner. He smoked good cigars, the ends of which he snipped off with a gold cigar-cutter, and his smile came readily, as from a man who had no fault to find with life. To continue the possibly unnecessary details, I may add further that whilst tenders were requested for the erection of the New Safe Deposit, the provision of the advertisement that the lowest tender would not necessarily be accepted was justified by the fact that the offer of Potham and Holloway was approved, and it is an open secret that their tender was the highest of all.

"My client requires the very best work; he desires a building that will stand shocks." Mr. Spedding shot a swift glance at the contractor, who sat at the other side of the desk. "Something that a footling little dynamite explosion would not scatter to the four winds."

The contractor nodded.

"You have read the specification," the solicitor went on—he was cutting a new cigar, "and in regard to the pedestal—ah—the pedestal, you know—?"

He stopped and looked at the contractor.

"It seems all very clear," said the great builder. He took a bundle of papers from an open bag by his side and read, "The foundation to be of concrete to the depth of twenty feet... The pedestal to be alternate layers of dressed granite and steel... in the centre a steel-lined compartment, ten inches by five, and half the depth of the pedestal itself."

The solicitor inclined his head. "That pedestal is to be the most important thing in the whole structure. The steel-lined recess—I don't know the technical phrase—which one of these days your men will have to fill in, is the second most important; but the safe that is to stand fifty feet above the floor of the building is to be—but the safe is arranged for."

An army of workmen, if the hackneyed phrase be permitted, descended upon Lombard Street and pulled down the old buildings. They pulled them down, and broke them down, and levered them down, and Lombard Street grew gray with dust. The interiors of quaint old rooms with grimy oak panelling were indecently exposed to a passing public. Clumsy, earthy carts blocked Lombard Street, and by night flaring Wells' lights roared amidst the chaos. And, bare-armed men sweated and delved by night and by day; and one morning Mr. Spedding stood in a drizzle of rain, with a silk umbrella over his head, and expressed, on behalf of his client, his intense satisfaction at the progress made. He stood on a slippery plank that formed a barrow road, and workmen, roused to unusual activity by the presence of "The Firm"—Mr. Spedding's cicerone—moved to and fro at a feverish rate of speed.

"They don't mind the rain," said the lawyer, sticking out his chin in the direction of the toiling gangs.

"The Firm" shook his head. "Extra pay," he said laconically, "we provided for that in the tender," he hastened to add in justification of his munificence.

So in rain and sunshine, by day and by night, the New Safe Deposit came into existence. Once—it was during a night shift—a brougham drove up the deserted city street, and a footman helped from the dark interior of the carriage a shivering old man with a white, drawn face. He showed a written order to the foreman, and was allowed inside the unpainted gate of the "works." He walked gingerly amidst the debris of construction, asked no questions, made no replies to the explanations of the bewildered foreman, who wondered what fascination there was in a building job to bring an old man from his bed at three o'clock on a chill spring morning.

Only once the old man spoke. "Where will that there pedestal be?" he asked in a harsh, cracked cockney voice; and when the foreman pointed out the spot, and the men even then busily filling in the foundation, the old man's lips curled back in an ugly smile that showed teeth too white and regular for a man of his age.

He said no more, but pulled the collar of his fur coat the tighter about his lean neck and walked wearily back to his carriage. The building saw Mr. Spedding's client no more—if, indeed, it was Mr. Spedding's client. So far as is known, he did not again visit Lombard Street before its completion—even when the last pane of glass had been fixed in the high gilded dome, when the last slab of marble had been placed in the ornate walls of the great hall, even when the solicitor came and stood in silent contemplation before the great granite pedestal that rose amidst a scaffolding of slim steel girders supporting a staircase that wound upward to the gigantic mid-air safe. Not quite alone, for with him was the contractor, awed to silence by the immensity of his creation.

"Finished!" said the contractor, and his voice came echoing back from the dim spaces of the building.

The solicitor did not answer.

"Your client may commence business tomorrow if he wishes."

The solicitor turned from the pedestal. "He is not ready yet," he said softly, as though afraid of the echoes. He walked to where the big steel doors of the hall stood ajar, the contractor following. In the vestibule he took two keys from his pocket. The heavy doors swung noiselessly across the entrance, and Mr. Spedding locked them. Through the vestibule and out into the busy street the two men walked, and the solicitor fastened behind him the outer doors.

"My client asks me to convey his thanks to you for your expedition," the lawyer said.

The builder rubbed his hands with some satisfaction.

"You have taken two days less than we expected," Mr. Spedding went on. The builder was a man of few ideas outside his trade.

He said again: "Yes, your client may start business tomorrow."

The solicitor smiled. "My client, Mr. Potham, may not—er—start business—for ten years," he said. "In fact, until—well, until he dies, Mr. Potham."

II. — THE HOUSE IN TERRINGTON SQUARE

A MAN turned into Terrington Square from Seymour Street and walked leisurely past the policeman on point duty, bidding him a curt "good night." The other subsequently described the passer, as a foreign-looking gentleman with a short pointed beard. Under the light overcoat he was apparently in evening dress, for the officer observed the shoes with the plain black bow, and the white silk muffler and the crush hat supported that view. The man crossed the road, and disappeared round the corner of the railed garden that forms the centre of the square. A belated hansom came jingling past, and an early newspaper cart, taking a short cut to Paddington, followed; then the square was deserted save for the man and the policeman. The grim, oppressive houses of the square werewrapped in sleep-drawn blinds and shuttered windows and silence.

The man continued his stroll until he came abreast of No. 43. Here he stopped for a second, gave one swift glance up and down the thoroughfare, and mounted the three steps of the house. He fumbled a little with the key, turned it, and entered. Inside he stood for a moment, then taking a small electric lamp from his pocket he switched on the current. He did not trouble to survey the wide entrance hall, but flashed the tiny beam of light on the inside face of the door. Two thin wires and a small coil fastened to the lintel called forth no comment. One of the wires had been snapped by the opening of the door.

"Burglar-alarm, of course," he murmured approvingly. "All the windows similarly treated, and goodness knows what pitfalls waiting for the unwary."

He flashed the lamp round the hall. A heavy Turkish rug at the foot of the winding staircase secured his attention. He took from his pocket a telescopic stick, extended it, and fixed it rigid. Then he walked carefully towards the rug. With his stick he lifted the corner, and what he saw evidently satisfied him, for he returned to the door, where in a recess stood a small marble statue. All his strength was required to lift this, but he staggered back with it, and rolling it on its circular base, as railway porters roll milk churns, he brought it to the edge of the rug. With la quick push he planted it square in the centre of the carpet. For a second only it stood,

5

oscillating, then like a flash it disappeared, and where the carpet had lain was a black, gaping hole.

He waited. Somewhere from the depths came a crash, and the carpet came slowly up again and filled the space. The unperturbed visitor nodded his head, as though again approving the householder's caution.

"I don't suppose he has learnt any new ones," he murmured regretfully," he is getting very old."

He took stock of the walls. They were covered with paintings and engravings.

"He could not have fixed the cross tire in a modern house," he continued, and taking a little run, leapt the rug and rested for a moment on the bottom stair. A suit of half armor on the first landing held him in thoughtful attention for a moment.

"Elizabethan body, with a Spanish bayonet," he said regretfully; "that doesn't look like a collector's masterpiece."

He flashed the lamp up and down the silent figure that stood in menacing attitude with a raised battle-axe.

"I don't like that axe," he murmured, and measured the distance.

Then he saw the fine wire that stretched across the landing. He stepped across carefully, and ranged himself alongside the steel knight. Slipping off his coat, he reached up and caught the figure by the wrist. Then with a quick jerk of his foot he snapped the wire. He had been prepared for the mechanical downfall of the axe; but as the wire broke the figure turned to the right, and swish! came the axe in a semicircular cut. He had thought to hold the arm as it descended, but he might as well have tried to hold the piston-rod of an engine. His hand was wrenched away, and the razor-like blade of the axe missed his head by the fraction of a second. Then with a whir the arm rose stiffly again to its original position and remained rigid.

The visitor moistened his lips and sighed.

"That's a new one, a very new one," he said under his breath, and the admiration in his tone was evident. He picked up his overcoat, flung it over his arm, and mounted half a dozen steps to the next landing. The inspection of the Chinese cabinet was satisfactory. The white beam of his lamp flashed into corners and crevices and showed nothing. He shook the curtain of a window and listened, holding his breath.

"Not here," he muttered decisively, "the old man wouldn't try that game. Snakes turned loose in a house in London, S.W., take a deal of collecting in the morning."

He looked round. From the landing access was gained to three rooms. That which from its position he surmised faced the street he did not attempt to enter. The second, covered by a heavy curtain, he looked at for a time in thought. To the third he walked, and carefully swathing the door-handle with his silk muffler, he turned it. The door yielded. He hesitated another moment, and jerking the door wide open, sprang backward. The interior of the room was for a second only in pitch darkness, save for the flicker of light that told of an open fireplace. Then the visitor heard a click, and the room was flooded with light. In the darkness on the landing the man waited; then a voice, a cracked old voice, said grumblingly:

"Come in." Still the man on the landing waited. "Oh, come in, Jimmy—I know ye."

Cautiously the man outside stepped through the entry into the light and faced the old man, who, arrayed in a wadded dressing-gown, sat in a big chair by the fire, an old man, with white face and a sneering grin, who sat with his lap full of papers. The visitor nodded a friendly greeting.

"As far as I can gather," he said deliberately, "we are just above your dressing-room, and if you dropped me through one of your patent traps, Reale, I should fetch up amongst your priceless china."

Save for a momentary look of alarm on the old man's face at the mention of the china, he preserved an imperturbable calm, never moving his eyes from his visitor's face. Then his grin returned, and he motioned the other to a chair on the other side of the fireplace.

Jimmy turned the cushion over with the point of his stick and sat down.

"Suspicious?" The grin broadened. "Suspicious of your old friend, Jimmy? The old governor, eh?"

Jimmy made no reply for a moment, then—"You're a wonder, governor, upon my word you are a wonder. That man in armour—your idea?"

The old man shook his head regretfully. "Not mine entirely, Jimmy. Ye see, there's electricity in it, and I don't know much about electricity, I never did, except—"

"Except?" suggested the visitor.

"Oh, that roulette board, that was my own idea; but that was magnetism, which is different to electricity, by my way of looking."

Jimmy nodded.

"Ye got past the trap?" The old man had just a glint of admiration in his eye.

"Yes, jumped it."

The old man nodded approvingly. "You always was a one for thinkin' things out. I've known lots of 'em who would never have thought of jumping it. Connor, and that pig Massey, they'd have walked right on to it. You didn't damage anything?" he demanded suddenly and fiercely. "I heard somethin' break, an' I was hoping that it was you." Jimmy thought of the marble statue, and remembered that it had looked valuable.

"Nothing at all," he lied easily, and the old man's tense look relaxed.

The pair sat on opposite sides of the fireplace, neither speaking for fully ten minutes; then Jimmy leant forward.

"Reale," he said quietly, "how much are you worth?"

In no manner disturbed by this leading question, but rather indicating a lively satisfaction, the other replied instantly: "Two millions an' a bit over, Jimmy. I've got the figures in my head. Reckonin' furniture and the things in this house at their proper value, two millions, and forty-seven thousand and forty-three pounds—floatin', Jimmy, absolute cash, the same as you might put your hand in your pocket an' spend—a million an' three—quarters exact."

He leant back in his chair with a triumphant grin and watched his visitor.

Jimmy had taken a cigarette from his pocket and was lighting it, looking at the slowly burning match reflectively.

"A million and three-quarters," he repeated calmly, "is a lot of money."

Old Reale chuckled softly.

"All made out of the confiding public, with the aid of me—and Connor and Massey-"

"Massey is a pig!" the old man interjected spitefully.

Jimmy puffed a cloud of tobacco smoke. "Wrung with sweat and sorrow from foolish young men who backed the tiger and played high at Reale's

Unrivalled Temple of Chance, Cairo, Egypt—with branches at Alexandria, Port Said, and Suez."

The figure in the wadded gown writhed in a paroxysm of silent merriment.

"How many men have you ruined, Reale?" asked Jimmy.

"The Lord knows," the old man answered cheerfully; "only three as I knows of—two of 'em's dead, one of 'em's dying. The two that's dead left neither chick nor child; the dying one's got a daughter."

Jimmy eyed him through narrowed lids. "Why this solicitude for the relatives—you're not going—?"

As he spoke, as if anticipating a question, the old man was nodding his head with feverish energy, and all the while his grin broadened.

"What a one you are for long words, Jimmy! You always was. That's how you managed to persuade your swell pals to come an' try their luck. Solicitude! What's that mean? Frettin' about 'em, d'ye mean? Yes, that's what I'm doin'—frettin' about 'em. And I'm going to make, what d'ye call it—you had it on the tip of your tongue a minute or two ago?"

"Reparation?" suggested Jimmy.

Old Reale nodded delightedly.

"How?"

"Don't you ask questions!" bullied the old man, his harsh voice rising. "I ain't asked you why you broke into my house in the middle of the night, though I knew it was you who came the other day to check the electric meter. I saw you, an' I've been waitin' for you ever since."

"I knew all about that," said Jimmy calmly, and flicked the ash of his cigarette away with his little finger, "and I thought you would—"

Suddenly he stopped speaking and listened.

"Who's in the house beside us?" he asked quickly, but the look on the old man's face reassured him.

"Nobody," said Reale testily. "I've got a special house for the servants, and they come in every morning after I've unfixed my burglar- alarms."

He grinned, and then a look of alarm came into his face.

"The alarms!" he whispered; "you broke them when you came in, Jimmy. I heard the signal. If there's some one in the house we shouldn't know it now."

They listened. Down below in the hall something creaked, then the sound of a soft thud came up.

"He's skipped the rug," whispered Jimmy, and switched out the light. The two men heard a stealthy footstep on the stair, and waited. There was the momentary glint of a light, and the sound of some one breathing heavily Jimmy leant over and whispered in the old man's ear. Then, as the handle of the door was turned and the door pushed open, Jimmy switched on the light.

The new-comer was a short, thick-set man with a broad, red face. He wore a check suit of a particularly glaring pattern, and on the back of his head was stuck a bowler hat, the narrow brim of which seemed to emphasize the breadth of his face. A casual observer might have placed him for a coarse, good—natured man of rude but boisterous humour. The ethnological student would have known him at once for what he was—a cruel man-beast without capacity for pity.

He started back as the lights went on, blinking a little, but his hand held an automatic pistol that covered the occupants of the room.

"Put up your hands," he growled. "Put 'em up!"

Neither man obeyed him. Jimmy was amused and looked it, stroking his short beard with his white tapering fingers. The old man was fury incarnate.

He it was that turned to Jimmy and croaked:

"What did I tell ye, Jimmy? What've I always said, Jimmy? Massey is a pig—he's got the manners of a pig. Faugh!"

"Put up your hands!" hissed the man with the pistol. "Put 'em up, or I'll put you both out!"

"If he'd come first, Jimmy!" Old Reale wrung his hands in his regret. "S'pose he'd jumped the rug—any sneak thief could have done that—d'ye think he'd have spotted the man in armor? If you'd only get the man in armor ready again."

"Put your pistol down, Massey," said Jimmy I coolly, "unless you want something to play with. Old man Reale's too ill for the gymnastics you suggest, and I'm not inclined to oblige you."

The man blustered. "By God, if you try any of your monkey tricks with me, either of you—"

"Oh, I'm only a visitor like yourself," said Jimmy, with a wave of his hand; "and as to monkey tricks, why, I could have shot you before you entered the room."

Massey frowned, and stood twiddling his pistol.

"You will find a safety catch on the left side of the barrel," continued Jimmy, pointing to the pistol; "snick it up—you can always push it down again with your thumb if you really mean business. You are not my idea of a burglar. You breathe too noisily, and you are built too clumsily; why, I heard you open the front door!"

The quiet contempt in the tone brought a deeper red into the man's face.

"Oh, you are a clever 'un, we know!" he began, and the old man, who had recovered his self-command, motioned him to a chair.

"Sit down, Mister Massey," he snapped; "sit down, my fine fellow, an' tell us all the news. Jimmy an' me was just speakin' about you, me an' Jimmy was. We was saying what a fine gentleman you was"—his voice grew shrill— "what a swine, what an overfed, lumbering fool of a pig you was, Mister Massey!"

He sank back into the depths of his chair exhausted.

"Look here, governor," began Massey again—he had laid his pistol on a table by his side, and waved a large red hand to give point to his remarks— "we don't want any unpleasantness. I've been a good friend to you, an' so has Jimmy. We've done your dirty work for years, me an' Jimmy have, and Jimmy knows it"—turning with an ingratiating smirk to the subject of his remarks—"and now we want a bit of our own—that is all it amounts to, our own."

Old Reale looked under his shaggy eyebrows to where Jimmy sat with brooding eyes watching the fire.

"So it's a plant, eh? You're both in it. Jimmy comes first, he being the clever one, an' puts the lay nice an' snug for the other feller."

Jimmy shook his head. "Wrong," he said. He turned his head and took a long scrutiny of the newcomer, and the amused contempt of his gaze was too apparent. "Look at him!" he said at last. "Our dear Massey! Does he look the sort of person I am likely to share confidence with?"

A cold passion seemed suddenly to possess him.

"It's a coincidence that brought us both together."

He rose and walked to where Massey sat, and stared down at him. There was something in the look that sent Massey's hand wandering to his pistol.

"Massey, you dog!" he began, then checked himself with a laugh and walked to the other end of the room. There was a tantalus with a soda siphon, and he poured himself a stiff portion and sent the soda fizzling into the tumbler. He held the glass to the light and looked at the old man. There was a look on the old man's face that he remembered to have seen before. He drank his whisky and gave utterance to old Reale's thoughts.

"It's no good, Reale, you've got to settle with Massey, but not the way you're thinking. We could put him away, but we should have to put ourselves away too." He paused. "And there's me," he added.

"And Connor," said Massey thickly, "and Connor's worse than me. I'm reasonable, Reale; I'd take a fair share—"

"You would, would you?" The old man was grinning again. "Well, your share's exactly a million an' three-quarters in solid cash, an' a bit over two millions—all in." He paused to notice the effect of his words. Jimmy's calm annoyed him; Massey's indifference was outrageous.

"An' it's Jimmy's share, an' Connor's share, an' it's Miss Kathleen Kent's share." This time the effect was better. Into Jimmy's inexpressive face had crept a gleam of interest.

"Kent?" he asked quickly. "Wasn't that the name of the man—?"

Old Reale chuckled. "The very feller, Jimmy—the man who came in to lose a tenner, an' lost ten thousand; who came in next night to get it back, and left his lot. That's the feller!"

He rubbed his lean hands, as at the memory of some pleasant happening.

"Open that cupboard, Jimmy." He pointed to an old—fashioned walnut cabinet that stood near the door. "D'ye see anything—a thing that looks like a windmill?"

Jimmy drew out a cardboard structure that was apparently a toy working-model. He handled it carefully, and deposited it on the table by the old man's side. Old Reale touched it caressingly. With his little finger he set a fly—wheel spinning, and tiny little pasteboard rods ran to and fro, and little wooden wheels spun easily.

"That's what I did with his money, invented a noo machine that went by itself—perpetual motion. You can grin, Massey, but that's what I did with it. Five years' work an' a quarter of a million, that's what that little model means. I never found the secret out. I could always make a machine that would go for hours with a little push, but it always wanted the push. I've been a chap that went in for inventions and puzzles. D'ye remember the table at Suez?"

He shot a sly glance at the men.

Massey was growing impatient as the reminiscences proceeded. He had come that night with an object; he had taken a big risk, and had not lost sight of the fact. Now he broke in—"Damn your puzzles, Reale. What about me; never mind about Jimmy. What's all this rotten talk about two millions for each of us, and this girl? When you broke up the place in Egypt you said we should stand in when the time came. Well, the time's come!"

"Nearly, nearly," said Reale, with his death's—head grin. "It's nearly come. You needn't have troubled to see me. My lawyer's got your addresses. I'm nearly through," he went on cheerfully; "dead I'll be in six months, as sure as—as death. Then you fellers will get the money"—he spoke slowly to give effect to his words—"you, Jimmy, or Massey or Connor or the young lady. You say you don't like puzzles, Massey? Well, it's a bad look out for you. Jimmy's the clever un, an' most likely he'll get it; Connor's artful, and he might get it from Jimmy; but the young lady's got the best chance, because women are good at puzzles."

"What in hell!" roared Massey, springing to his feet.

"Sit down!" It was Jimmy that spoke, and Massey obeyed.

"There's a puzzle about these two millions," Reale went on, and his croaky voice, with its harsh cockney accent, grew raucous in his enjoyment of Massey's perplexity and Jimmy's knit brows. "An' the one that finds the puzzle out, gets the money."

Had he been less engrossed in his own amusement he would have seen a change in Massey's brute face that would have warned him.

"It's in my will," he went on. "I'm goin' to set the sharps against the flats; the touts of the gamblin' hell—that's you two fellers—against the pigeons.

Two of the biggest pigeons is dead, an' one's dying. Well, he's got a daughter; let's see what she can do. When I'm dead—"

"That's now!" bellowed Massey, and leant over and struck the old man.

Jimmy, on his feet, saw the gush of blood and the knife in Massey's hand, and reached for his pocket. Massey's pistol covered him, and the man's face was a dreadful thing to look upon.

"Hands up! It's God's truth I'll kill you if you don't!" Jimmy's hands went up.

"He's got the money here," breathed Massey, "somewhere in this house."

"You're mad," said the other contemptuously. "Why did you hit him?"

"He sat there makin' a fool of me." The murderer gave a vicious glance at the inert figure on the floor. "I want something more than his puzzle-talk. He asked for it."

He backed to the table where the decanter stood, and drank a tumbler half-filled with raw spirit.

"We're both in this, Jimmy," he said, still keeping his man covered. "You can put down your hands; no monkey tricks. Give me your pistol."

Jimmy slipped the weapon from his pocket, and handed it butt foremost to the man. Then Massey bent over the fallen man and searched his pockets.

"Here are the keys. You stay here," said Massey, and went out, closing the door after him. Jimmy heard the grate of the key, and knew he was a prisoner. He bent over the old man. He lay motionless. Jimmy tried the pulse, and felt a faint flutter. Through the clenched teeth he forced a little whisky, and after a minute the old man's eyes opened.

"Jimmy!" he whispered; then remembering, "Where's Massey?" he asked. There was no need to inquire the whereabouts of Massey. His blundering footfalls sounded in the room above.

"Lookin' for money?" gasped the old man, and something like a smile crossed his face. "Safe's up there," he whispered, and smiled again. "Got the keys?"

Jimmy nodded. The old man's eyes wandered round the room till they rested on what looked like a switchboard.

"See that handle marked 'seven'?" he whispered. Jimmy nodded again. "Pull it down, Jimmy boy." His voice was growing fainter. "This is a new one that I read in a book. Pull it down."

"Why?"

"Do as I tell you," the lips motioned, and Jimmy walked across the room and pulled over the insulated lever.

As he did there was a heavy thud overhead that shook the room, and then silence.

"What's that?" he asked sharply. The dying man smiled.

"That's Massey!" said the lips.

Half an hour later Jimmy left the house with a soiled slip of paper in his waistcoat pocket, on which was written the most precious verse of doggerel that the world has known. And the discovery of the two dead men in the upper chambers the next morning afforded the evening press the sensation of the year.

IV. — ANGEL ESQUIRE

Nobody quite knows how Angel Esquire came to occupy the position he does at Scotland Yard. On his appointment, "An Officer of Twenty Years' Standing" wrote to the Police Review and characterized the whole thing as "a job."

Probably it was. For Angel Esquire had been many things in his short but useful career, but never a policeman. He had been a big game shot, a special correspondent, a "scratch" magistrate, and his nearest approach to occupying a responsible position in any police force in the world was when he was appointed a J.P. of Rhodesia, and, serving on the Tuli Commission, he hanged M'Linchwe and six of that black desperado's companions.

His circle of acquaintances extended to the suburbs of London, and the suburbanites, who love you to make their flesh creep, would sit in shivering but pleasurable horror whilst Angel Esquire elaborated the story of the execution.

In Mayfair Angel Esquire was best known as a successful mediator.

"Who is that old-looking young man with the wicked eye?" asked the Dowager Duchess of Hoeburn; and her vis-a-vis at the Honorable Mrs. Carter-Walker's "sit-down tea"—it was in the days when Mayfair was aping suburbia—put up his altogether unnecessary eyeglass.

"Oh, that's Angel Esquire!" he said carelessly. "What is he?" asked the Duchess. "A policeman." "India?" "Oh, no, Scotland Yard."

"Good Heavens!" said Her Grace in a shocked voice. "How very dreadful! What is he doing? Watching the guests, or keeping a friendly eye on the Carter woman's spoons?"

The young man guffawed. "Don't despise old Angel, Duchess," he said. "He's a man to know. Great fellow for putting things right. If you have a row with your governor, or get into the hands of—er—undesirables, or generally, if you're in a mess of any kind, Angel's the chap to pull you out"

Her Grace surveyed the admirable man with a new interest.

Angel Esquire, with a cup of tea in one hand und a thin grass sandwich in the other, was the centre of a group of men, including the husband of the hostess. He was talking with some animation.

"I held three aces pat, and opened the pot light to let 'em in. Young Saville raised the opening a tenner, and the dealer went ten better. George Manfred, who had passed, came in for a pony, and took one card. I took two, and drew another ace. Saville took one, and the dealer stood pat. I thought it was my money, and bet a pony. Saville raised it to fifty, the dealer made it a hundred, and George Manfred doubled the bet. It was up to me. I had four aces; I put Saville with a 'full,' and the dealer with a "flush." I had the beating of that lot; but what about Manfred? Manfred is a feller with all the sense going. He knew what the others had. If he bet, he had the goods, so I chucked my four aces into the discard. George had a straight flush."

A chorus of approval came from the group. If "An Officer of Twenty Years' Standing" had been a listener, he might well have been further strengthened in his opinion that of all persons Mr. Angel was least fitted to fill the responsible position he did.

If the truth be told, nobody quite knew exactly what position Angel did hold.

If you turn into New Scotland Yard and ask the janitor at the door for Mr. Christopher Angel—Angel Esquire by the way was a nickname affixed by a pert little girl—the constable, having satisfied himself as to your bona fides, would take you up a flight of stairs and hand you over to yet another officer, who would conduct you through innumerable swing doors, and along uncounted corridors till he stopped before a portal inscribed "647." Within, you would find Angel Esquire sitting at his desk, doing nothing, with the aid of a Sporting Life and a small weekly guide to the Turf.

Once Mr. Commissioner himself walked into the room unannounced, and found Angel so immersed in an elaborate calculation, with big sheets of paper closely filled with figures, and open books on either hand, that he did not hear his visitor.

"What is the problem?" asked Mr. Commissioner, and Angel looked up with his sweetest smile, and recognizing his visitor, rose.

"What's the problem?" asked Mr. Commissioner again.

"A serious flaw, sir," said Angel, with all gravity. "Here's Mimosa handicapped at seven stone nine in the Friary Nursery, when, according to my calculations, she can give the field a stone, and beat any one of 'em."

The Commissioner gasped. "My dear fellow," he expostulated, "I thought you were working on the Lagos Bank business."

Angel had a far-away look in his eyes when he answered—"Oh, that is all finished. Old Carby was poisoned by a man named—forget his name now, but he was a Monrovian. I wired the Lagos police, and we caught the chap this morning at Liverpool—took him off an Elder, Dempster boat."

The Police Commissioner beamed. "My congratulations, Angel. By Jove, I thought we shouldn't have a chance of helping the people in Africa. Is there a white man in it?"

"We don't know," said Angel absently his eye was wandering up and down a column of figures on the paper before him. "I am inclined to fancy there is—man named Connor, who used to be a croupier or something to old Reale."

He frowned at the paper, and picking up a pencil from the desk, made a rapid little calculation.

"Seven stone thirteen," he muttered.

The Commissioner tapped the table impatiently. He had sunk into a seat opposite Angel.

"My dear man, who is old Reale? You forget that you are our tame foreign specialist. Lord, Angel, if you heard half the horrid things that people say about your appointment you would die of shame!"

Angel pushed aside the papers with a little laugh.

"I'm beyond shame," he said light-heartedly; "and, besides, I've heard. you were asking about Reale. Reale is a character. For twenty years proprietor of one of the most delightful gambling plants in Egypt, Rome— goodness knows where. Education—none. Hobbies—invention. That's the 'bee in his bonnet'—invention. If he's got another, it is the common or garden puzzle. Pigs in clover, missing words, all the fake competitions that cheap little papers run—he goes in for them all. Lives at 43 Terrington Square."

"Where?" The Commissioner's eyebrows rose. "Reale? 43 Terrington Square? Why, of course."

He looked at Angel queerly. "You know all about Reale?"

Angel shrugged his shoulders: "As much as anybody knows," he said.

The Commissioner nodded. "Well, take a cab and get down at once to 43 Terrington Square: Your old Reale was murdered last night."

It was peculiar of Angel Esquire that nothing surprised him. He received the most tremendous tidings with polite interest, and now he merely said, "Dear me!"

Later, as a swift hansom carried him along Whitehall he permitted himself to be "blessed."

Outside No. 43 Terrington Square a small crowd of morbid sightseers stood in gloomy anticipation of some gruesome experience or other.

A policeman admitted him, and the local inspector stopped in his interrogation of a white-faced butler bid him a curt "Good morning." Angel's preliminary inspection did not take any time. He saw the bodies, which had not yet been removed. He examined the pockets of both men, und ran his eye through the scattered papers on the floor of the room in which the tragedy had occurred. Then he came back to the big drawing-room and saw the inspector, who was sitting at a table writing his report.

"The chap on the top floor committed the murder, of course," said Angel.

"I know that," said Inspector Boyden brusquely.

"And was electrocuted by a current passing through the handle of the safe."

"I gathered that," the inspector replied as before, and went on with his work.

"The murderer's name is Massey," continued Angel patiently, "George Charles Massey."

The inspector turned in his seat with a sarcastic smile. "I also," he said pointedly, "have seen the envelopes addressed in that name, which were found in his pocket."

Angel's face was preternaturally solemn as he continued—"The third man I am not so sure about."

The inspector looked up suspiciously. "Third man—which third man?"

Well—simulated astonishment sent Angel's eye-brows to the shape of inverted V's.

"There was another man in it. Didn't you know that, Mr. Inspector?"

"I have found no evidence of the presence of a third party," he said stiffly; "but I have not yet concluded my investigations."

"Good!" said Angel cheerfully. "When you have, you will find the ends of three cigarettes—two in the room where the old man was killed, and one in the safe room. They are marked 'Al Kam,' and are a fairly expensive variety of Egyptian cigarettes. Massey smoked cigars; old Reale did not smoke at all. The question is"—he went on speaking aloud to himself, and ignoring the perplexed police official—"was it Connor or was it Jimmy?"

The inspector struggled with a desire to satisfy his curiosity at the expense of his dignity, and resolved to maintain an attitude of superior incredulity.

He turned back to his work.

"It would be jolly difficult to implicate either of them," Angel went on reflectively, addressing the back of the inspector. "They would produce fifty unimpeachable alibis, and bring an action for wrongful arrest in addition," he added artfully.

"They can't do that," said the inspector gruffly.

"Can't they?" asked the innocent Angel. "Well, at any rate, it's not advisable to arrest them. Jimmy would—"

Inspector Boyden swung round in his chair. "I don't know whether you're 'pulling my leg,' Mr. Angel. You are perhaps unused to the procedure in criminal cases in London, and I must now inform you that at present I am in charge of the ease, and must request that if you have any information bearing upon this crime to give it to me at once."

"With all the pleasure in life," said Angel heartily. "In the first place, Jimmy—"

"Full name, please." The inspector dipped his pen in ink.

"Haven't the slightest idea," said the other carelessly. "Everybody knows Jimmy. He was old Reale's most successful decoy duck. Had the presence and the plumage and looked alive, so that all the other little ducks used to come flying down and settle about him, and long before they could discover that the beautiful bird that attracted them was only painted wood and feathers, 'Bang! bang!' went old Reale's double-barrel, and roast duck was on the menu for days on end."

Inspector Boyden threw down his pen with a grunt. "I'm afraid," he said in despair, "that I cannot include your parable in my report. When you have any definite information to give, I shall be pleased to receive it."

Later, at Scotland Yard, Angel interviewed the Commissioner. "What sort of a man is Boyden to work with?" asked Mr. Commissioner.

"A most excellent chap—good-natured, obliging, and as zealous as the best of 'em," said Angel, which was his way.

"I shall leave him in charge of the case," said the Chief.

"You couldn't do better," said Angel decisively.

Then he went home to his flat in Jermyn Street to dress for dinner. It was an immaculate Angel Esquire who pushed through the plate-glass, turntable door of the Heinz, and, walking into the magnificent old rose dining-room, selected a table near a window looking out on to Piccadilly.

The other occupant of the table looked up and nodded.

"Hullo, Angel!" he said easily.

"Hullo, Jimmy!" greeted the unconventional detective. He took up the card and chose his dishes with elaborate care. A half-bottle of Beaujolais completed his order.

"The ridiculous thing is that one has got to pay 7s. 6d. for a small bottle of wine that any respectable grocer will sell you for tenpence ha'penny net."

"You must pay for the magnificence," said the other, quietly amused. Then, after the briefest pause, "What do you want?"

"Not you, Jimmy," said the amiable Angel, "though my young friend, Boyden, Inspector of Police, and a Past Chief Templar to boot, will be looking for you shortly."

Jimmy carefully chose a toothpick and stripped it of its tissue covering.

"Of course," he said quietly, "I wasn't in it—the killing, I mean. I was there."

"I know all about that," said Angel; "saw your foolish cigarettes. I didn't think you had any hand in the killing. You are a I property criminal, not a personal criminal."

"By which I gather you convey the nice distinction as between crimes against property and crimes against the person," said the other.

"Exactly." A pause. "Well?" said Jimmy.

"What I want to see you about is the verse," said Angel, stirring his soup.

Jimmy laughed aloud. "What a clever little devil you are, Angel," he said admiringly; "and not so little either, in inches or devilishness."

He relapsed into silence, and the wrinkled forehead was eloquent.

"Think hard," taunted Angel.

"I'm thinking," said Jimmy slowly. "I used a pencil, as there was no blotting paper. I only made one copy, just as the old man dictated it, and—"

"You used a block," said Angel obligingly, "and only tore off the top sheet. And you pressed rather heavily on that, so that the next sheet bore a legible impression."

Jimmy looked annoyed. "What an ass I am !" he said, and was again silent.

"The verse?" said Angel. "Can you make head or tail of it?"

"No"—Jimmy shook his head—"can you?"

"Not a blessed thing," Angel frankly confessed.

Through the next three courses neither man spoke. When coffee had been placed on the table, Jimmy broke the silence—"You need not worry about the verse. I have only stolen a march of a few days. Then Connor will have it; and some girl or other will have it. Massey would have had it too." He smiled grimly.

"What is it all about?"

Jimmy looked at his questioner with some suspicion. "Don't you know?" he demanded.

"Haven't got the slightest notion. That is why I came to see you."

"Curious!" mused Jimmy. "I thought of looking you up for the very same purpose. We'll all know in a day or two," he went on, beckoning the waiter.

"The old man said it was all in the will. He just told me the verse before he died. The ruling passion, don't you know. 'Learn it by heart, Jimmy,' he croaked; 'it's two millions for you if you guess it' '-and that's how he died. My bill, waiter. Which way do you go?" he asked as they turned into Piccadilly.

"To the 'Plait' for an hour," said Angel.

"Business?"

"Partly; I'm looking for a man who might be there."

They crossed Piccadilly, and entered a side turning. The second on the left and the first on the right brought them opposite a brightly-lit hotel. From within came the sound of violins. At the little tables with which the spacious bar-room was set about sat laughing women and young men in evening dress. A haze of cigarette smoke clouded the atmosphere, and the music made itself heard above a babel of laughter and talk. They found a corner, and seated themselves.

"You seem to be fairly well known here," said Jimmy.

"Yes," replied Angel ruefully, "a jolly sight too well known. You're not quite a stranger, Jimmy," he added.

"No," said the other a little bitterly; "but we're on different sides of the House, Angel. You're in the Cabinet, and I'm in the everlasting Opposition."

"Muffled sobs!" said Angel flippantly. "Pity poor Ishmael who 'ishes' for his own pleasure! Pathos for a fallen brother! A silent tear for this magnificent wreck who'd rather be on the rocks than floating any day of the week. Don't humbug yourself, Jimmy, or I shall be falling on your neck and appealing to your better nature. You're a thief just as another man is a stamp collector or a hunter. It's your blooming forte. Hi, Charles, do you ever intend serving me?"

"Yessir; d'reckly, sir" Charles bustled up. "What is it to be, gentlemen? Good evening, Mr. Angel!"

"I'll take what my friend Dooley calls a keg of obscenth; and you?"

Jimmy's face struggled to preserve its gravity. "Lemonade," he said soberly. The waiter brought him a whisky. If you do not know the "Plait" you do not know your London. It is one of the queer hostels which in a Continental city would be noted as a place to which the "young person" might not be taken. Being in London, neither Baedeker nor any of the infallible guides to the metropolis so much as mention its name. For there is a law of libel.

"There's 'Snatch' Walker," said Angel idly. "Snatch isn't wanted just now—in this country. There's 'Frisco Kate,' who'll get a lifer one of these days. D'ye know the boy in the mustard suit, Jimmy?"

Jimmy took a sidelong glance at the young man. "No; he's new."

"Not so new either," said Angel. "Budapest in the racing season, Jerusalem in the tourist season; a wealthy Hungarian nobleman travelling for his health all the time—that's him."

"Ambiguous, ungrammatical, but convincing," murmured Jimmy.

"I want him, by the way!" Angel had suddenly become alert.

"If you're going to have a row, I'm off," said Jimmy, finishing his drink.

Angel caught his arm. A man had entered the saloon, and was looking round as though in search of somebody. He caught Jimmy's eye and started. Then he threaded his way through the crowded room.

"Hullo, Jim—'" He stopped dead as he saw Jimmy's companion, and his hand went into his pocket.

"Hullo, Connor!" Angel's smile was particularly disarming. "You're the man I want to see."

"What's the game?" the other snarled. He was a big, heavily-built man, with a drooping moustache.

"Nothing, nothing," smiled Angel. "I want you for the Lagos job, but there's not enough evidence to convict you. Make your mind easy."

The man went white under his tan; his hand caught the edge of the table before him. "Lagos!" he stammered. "What—what—"

"Oh, never mind about that." Angel airily waved the matter aside. "Sit down here."

The man hesitated, then obeyed, and dropped into a seat between the two. Angel looked round. So far as any danger of being overheard went, they were as much' alone as though they sat in the centre of a desert.

"Jimmy"—Angel held him by the arm—"you said just now you'd got a march when you admitted you'd seen old Reale's puzzle verse. It wasn't the march you thought it was, for I had seen the will—and so has Connor here."

He looked the heavy man straight in the eye. "There is somebody else that benefits under that will besides you two. It is a girl."

He did not take his eyes from Connor. "I was curious to see that young lady," Angel went on, "and this afternoon I drove to CIapham to interview her." He stopped again. Connor made no reply, but kept his eyes fixed on the floor.

"I went to interview her, and found that she had mysteriously disappeared this very afternoon." Again he stopped. "A gentleman called to see her, with a message from—who do you think, Connor?" he asked.

The easy, flippant manner was gone, and Connor looking up, caught the steady stare of two wild blue eyes, and shivered.

"Why," Angel went on slowly, "it was a message from Inspector Angel—which is a damned piece of impudence, Connor, for I'm not an inspector—and the young lady drove away to Scotland Yard. And now, Connor, I want to ask you, What have you done with old Reale's heiress?"

Connor licked his lips and said nothing.

Angel beckoned to a waiter and paid his score, then rose to go.

"You will go at once and drive Miss Kathleen Kent back to the place you took her from. I shall call tomorrow and see her, and if one hair of her head is harmed, Connor—"

"Well?" said Connor defiantly.

"I'll chance your alibis, and take you for the Lagos business," and with a curt nod to Jimmy, he left the saloon.

Connor turned in a fret of fury to the man at his side. "D'ye hear him, Jimmy? D'ye hear the dog—"

"My advice to you," interrupted the other, "is—do as Angel tells you."

"D'ye think I'm frightened by—"

"Oh, no," was the quiet response, "you are not frightened at what Angel may do. What he does won't matter very much. What I will do is the trouble."

IV. — THE "BOROUGH LOT"

IT was not a bit like Scotland Yard as Kathleen Kent had pictured it. It was a kind of a yard certainly, for the grimy little street, flanked on either side with the blank faces of dirty little houses, ended abruptly in a high wall, over which were the gray hulls and fat scarlet funnels of ocean-going steamers. The driver of the cab had pulled up before one of the houses near the wall, and a door had opened. Then the man who had sat with her in glum silence, answering her questions in monosyllables, grasped her arm and hurried her into the house. The door slammed behind, and she realized her deadly peril.

She had had a foreboding, an instinctive premonition that all was not well when the cab had turned from the broad thoroughfare that led to where she had imagined Scotland Yard would be, and had, taking short cuts through innumerable me an streets, moved at a sharp pace eastward. Ignorant of that London which begins at Trafalgar Square and runs eastward to Walthamstow, ignorant, indeed, of that practical suburb to which the modesty of an income produced by 4,000 pounds worth of Consols had relegated her, she felt without knowing, that Scotland Yard did not lay at the eastern end of Commercial Road. Then when the door of the little house slammed and a hand grasped her arm tightly, and a thick voice whispered in her ear that if she screamed the owner of the voice would "out" her, she gathered, without exactly knowing what an "outing" was, that it would be wiser for her not to scream, so she quietly accompanied her captor up the stairs. He stopped for a moment on the rickety landing, then pushed open a door. Before the window that would in the ordinary course of events admit the light of day hung a heavy green curtain; behind this, though she did not know it, three army blankets, judiciously fixed, effectively excluded the sunlight, and as effectually veiled the rays of a swing-lamp from outside observation.

The girl made a pathetically incongruous figure, as she stood white, but resolute before the occupants of the room.

Kathleen Kent was something more than pretty, something less than beautiful. An oval face with gray, steadfast eyes, a straight nose and the narrow upper lip of the aristocrat, her lips were, perhaps, too full and too human for your connoisseur of beauty.

She looked from face to face, and but for her pallor she exhibited no sign of fear. Although she was unaware of the fact, she had been afforded an extraordinary privilege. By the merest accident, she had been ushered into the presence of the "Borough Lot." Not a very heroic title for an organized band of criminals, but, then, organized criminals never take unto themselves generic and high-falutin' titles. Our "Silver Hatchets" and "Red Knives" are boy hooligans who shoot off toy pistols. The police referred to them vaguely as the "Borough Lot". Lesser lights in the criminal world have been known to boast that they were not unconnected with that combination; and when some desperate piece of villainy startled the world, the police investigating the crime started from this point: Was it committed by one of the Borough Lot, or was it not?

As Kathleen was pushed into the room by her captor, a hum of subdued conversation ended abruptly, and she was the focus of nine pairs of passionless eyes that looked at her unsmilingly. When she had heard the voices, when she took her first swift glance at the room, and had seen the type of face that met hers, she had steeled herself for an outburst of coarse amusement. She feared—she did not know what she feared. Strangely enough, the dead silence that greeted her gave her courage, the cold stare of the men nerved her. Only one of the men lost his composure. The tall, heavy-looking man who sat at one end of the room with bowed, attentive head listening to a little clean-shaven man with side-whiskers, who looked for all the world like an old-fashioned jockey, started with a muttered oath.

"Upstairs!" he roared, and said something rapidly in a foreign tongue that sent the man who held the girl's arm staggering back with a blanched face. "I... I..." he stammered appealingly, "I didn't understand."

The tall man, his face flushed with rage, pointed to the door, and hastily opening the door, her captor half dragged the bewildered girl to the darkness of the landing.

"This way," he muttered, and she could feel his hand trembling as he stumbled up yet another flight of stairs, never once relinquishing his hold of her.

"Don't you scream nor nothing, or you'll get into trouble. You see what happened to me for takin' you into the wrong room. Oh, he's a devil is Connor—Smith, I mean. Smith's his name, d'ye hear?"

He shook her arm roughly. Evidently the man was beside himself with terror. What dreadful thing the tall man had said, Kathleen could only judge. She herself was half dead with fright. The sinister faces of these men, the mystery of this assembly in the shuttered room, her abduction, all combined to add terror to her position.

Her conductor unlocked a door and pushed her in. This had evidently been prepared for her reception, for a table had been laid, and food and drink stood ready. The door was closed behind her, and a bolt was slipped. Like the chamber below, all daylight was kept out by a curtain. Her first thoughts were of escape.

She waited till the footsteps on the rickety stairs had died away, then crossed the room swiftly. The drop from the window could not be very far; she would risk it. She drew aside the curtain. Where the window should have been was a sheet of steel plate. It was screwed to the joists. Somebody had anticipated her resolve to escape by the window. In chalk, written in an illiterate hand, was the sentence:

"You wont be hert if your senserble. We want to know some questions then well let you go. Don't make a fuss or it will be bad for you. Keep quite and tell us these questions and well let you go."

What had they to ask, or she to answer? She knew of nothing that she could inform them upon. Who were these men who were detaining her? During the next hours she asked herself these questions over and over again. She grew faint with hunger and thirst, but the viands spread upon the table she did not touch. The mystery of her capture bewildered her. Of what value was she to these men? All the time the murmur of voices in the room below was continuous. Once or twice she heard a voice raised in anger. Once a door slammed, and somebody went clattering down the stairs. There was a doorkeeper, she could hear him speak with the outgoer.

Did she but know it, the question that perplexed her was an equal matter of perplexity with others in the house that evening. The notorious men upon whom she had looked, all innocent of their claim to notoriety, were themselves puzzled. Bat Sands, the man who looked so ill—he had the unhealthy appearance of one who had just come through a long sickness— was an inquirer, Vinnis—nobody knew his Christian name—was another, and they were two men whose inquiries were not to be put off.

Vinnis turned his dull fish eyes upon big Connor, and spoke with deliberation. "Connor, what's this girl business? Are we in it?"

Connor knew his men too well to temporize. "You're in it, if it's worth anything," he said slowly.

Bat's close-cropped red head was thrust forward. "Is there money in it?" he demanded.

Connor nodded his head.

"Much?" Connor drew a deep breath. If the truth be told, that the "Lot" should share, was the last thing he had intended. But for the blundering of his agent, they would have remained in ignorance of the girl's presence in the house. But the very suspicion of disloyalty was dangerous. He knew his men, and they knew him. There was not a man there who would hesitate to destroy him at the merest hint of treachery. Candour was the best and safest course.

"It's pretty hard to give you any idea what I've got the girl here for, but there's a million in it," he began.

He knew they believed him. He did not expect to be disbelieved. Criminals of the class these men represented flew high. They were out of the ruck of petty, boasting sneak-thieves who lied to one another, knowing they lied, and knowing that their hearers knew they lied. Only the strained, intent look on their faces gave any indication of how the news had been received.

"It's old Reale's money," he continued; "he's left the lot to four of us, Massey's dead, so that makes three." There was no need to explain who was Reale, who Massey. A week ago Massey had himself sat in that room and discussed with Connor the cryptic verse that played so strange a part in the old man's will. He had been, in a way, an honorary member of the "Borough Lot."

Connor continued. He spoke slowly, waiting for inspiration. A judicious lie might save the situation. But no inspiration came, and he found his reluctant tongue speaking the truth.

"The money is stored in one safe. Oh, it's no use looking like that, Tony, you might just as well try to crack the Bank of England as that crib. Yes, he converted every cent of a million and three-quarters into hard, solid cash—banknotes and gold. This he put into his damned safe, and locked. And he has left by the terms of his will a key."

Connor was a man who did not find speaking an easy matter. Every word came slowly and hesitatingly, as though the speaker of the story were loth to part with it.

"The key is here," he said slowly. There was a rustle of eager anticipation as he dipped his hand in his waistcoat pocket. When he withdrew his fingers, they contained only a slip of paper carefully folded.

"The lock of the safe is one of Reale's inventions; it opens to no key save this."

He hook the paper before them, then lapsed into silence.

"Well," broke in Bat impatiently, "why don't you open the safe? And what has the girl to do with it?"

"She also has a key, or will have tomorrow. And Jimmy ... "

A laugh interrupted him. "Curt" Goyle had been an attentive listener till Jimmy's name was mentioned, then his harsh, mirthless laugh broke the tense silence.

"Oh, Lord James is in it, is he? I'm one that's for ruling Jimmy out."

He got up on his feet and stretched himself, keeping his eye fixed on Connor.

"If you want to know why, I'll tell ye. Jimmy's a bit too finicking for my taste, too fond of the police for my taste. If we're in this, Jimmy's out of it," and a mutter of approval broke from the men.

Connor's mind was working quickly. He could do without Jimmy, he could not dispense with the help of the "Lot." He was just a little afraid of Jimmy. The man was a type of criminal he could not understand. If he was a rival claimant for Reale's millions, the gang would "out" Jimmy; so much the better. Massey's removal had limited the legatees to three. Jimmy out of the way would narrow the chance of his losing the money still further; and the other legatee was in the room upstairs. Goyle's declaration had set loose the tongues of the men, and he could hear no voice that spoke for Jimmy. And then a dozen voices demanded the rest of the story, and amid a dead silence Connor told the story of the will and the puzzle-verse, the solving of which meant fortune to every man.

"And the girl has got to stand in and take her share. She's too dangerous to be let loose. There's nigh on two millions at stake and I'm taking no risks. She shall remain here till the word is found. We're not going to see her carry off the money under our very noses."

"And Jimmy?" Goyle asked.

Connor fingered a lapel of his coat nervously. He knew what answer the gang had already framed to the question Goyle put. He knew he would be asked to acquiesce in the blackest piece of treachery that had ever disfigured his evil life; but he knew, too, that Jimmy was hated by the men who formed this strange fraternity. Jimmy worked alone; he shared neither risk nor reward. His cold cynicism was above their heads. They too feared him.

Connor cleared his throat. "Perhaps if we reasoned—"

Goyle and Bat exchanged swift glances. "Ask him to come and talk it over tonight," said Goyle carelessly.

"Connor is a long time gone." Sands turned his unhealthy face to the company as he spoke. Three hours had passed since Connor had left the gang in his search for Jimmy.

"He'll be back soon," said Goyle confidently. He looked over the assembly of men. "Any of you fellers who don't want to be in this business can go."

Then he added significantly, "We're going to settle with Jimmy."

Nobody moved; no man shuddered at the dreadful suggestion his words conveyed. "A million an' three-quarters—it's worth hanging for!" he said callously.

He walked to a tall, narrow cupboard that ran up by the side of the fireplace and pulled open the door. There was room for a man to stand inside. The scrutiny of the interior gave him some satisfaction. "This is where some one stood"—he looked meaningly at Bat Sand—"when he coshed Ike Steen—Ike with the police money in his pocket, and ready to sell every man jack of you."

"Who's in the next house?" a voice asked suddenly. Goyle laughed. He was the virtual landlord so far as the hiring of the house was concerned. He closed the cupboard door. "Not counting old George, it's empty," he said. "Listen!"

In the deep silence there came the faint murmur of a voice through the thin walls. "Talkin' to himself," said Goyle with a grin; "he's daft, and he's as good as a watchman for us, or he scares away the children and women who would come prying about here. He's—"

They heard the front door shut quickly and the voices of two men in the passage below.

Goyle sprang to his feet, an evil look on his face. "That's Jimmy!" he whispered hurriedly. As the feet sounded on the stairs he walked to where his coat hung and took something from his pocket, then, almost as the newcomers entered the room, he slipped into the cupboard and drew the door close after him.

Jimmy entering the room in Connor's wake, felt the chill of his reception. He felt, too, some indefinable sensation of danger. There was an ominous quiet. Bat Sands was polite, even servile. Jimmy noticed that, and his every sense became alert. Bat thrust forward a chair and placed it with its back toward the cupboard.

"Sit down, Jimmy," he said with forced heartiness. "We want a bit of a talk."

Jimmy sat down. "I also want a bit of a talk," he said calmly. "There is a young lady in this house, brought here against her will. You've got to let her go."

The angry mutter of protest that he had expected did not come, rather was his dictum received in complete silence. This was bad, and he looked round for the danger. Then he missed a face.

"Where is our friend Goyle, our dear landlord?" he asked with pleasant irony.

"He hasn't been here today," Bat hastened to say.

Jimmy looked at Connor standing by the door biting his nails, and Connor avoided his eye.

"Ah!" Jimmy's unconcern was perfectly simulated.

"Jimmy wants us to send the girl back." Connor was speaking hurriedly. "He thinks there'll be trouble, and his friend the 'tec thinks there will be trouble too."

Jimmy heard the artfully-worded indictment unmoved. Again he noticed, with some concern, that what was tantamount to a charge of treachery was received without a word.

"It isn't what others think, it is what I think, Connor," he said dryly. "The girl has got to go back. I want Reale's money as much as you, but I have a fancy to play fair this journey."

"Oh, you have, have you," sneered Connor. He had seen the cupboard door behind Jimmy move ever so slightly. Jimmy sat with his legs crossed on the chair that had been placed for him. The light overcoat he had worn over his evening dress lay across his knees. Connor knew the moment was at hand, and concentrated his efforts to keep his former comrade's attentions engaged. He had guessed the meaning of Goyle's absence from the room and the moving cupboard door. In his present position Jimmy was helpless. Connor had been nervous to a point of incoherence on the way to the house.

Now his voice rose to a strident pitch.

"You're too clever, Jimmy," he said, "and there are too many 'musts' about you to please us. We say that the girl has got to stay, and by—we mean it!"

Jimmy's wits were at work. The danger was very close at hand, he felt that. He must change his tactics. He had depended too implicitly upon Connor's fear of him, and had reckoned without the "Borough Lot".

From which of these men did danger threaten? He took their faces in in one comprehensive glance. He knew them—he had their black histories at his fingertips. Then he saw a coat hanging on the wall at the farther end of the room. He recognized the garment instantly. It was Goyle's. Where was the owner? He temporized.

"I haven't the slightest desire to upset anybody's plans," he drawled, and started drawing on a white glove, as though about to depart. "I am willing to hear your views, but I would point out that I have an equal interest in the young lady, Connor."

He gazed reflectively into the palm of his gloved hand as if admiring the fit. There was something so peculiar in this apparently innocent action, that Connor started forward with an oath.

"Quick, Goyle!" he shouted; but Jimmy was out of his chair and was standing with his back against the cupboard, and in Jimmy's ungloved hand was an ugly black weapon that was all butt and barrel.

He waved them back, and they shrank away from him.

"Let me see you all," he commanded, "none of your getting behind one another. I want to see what you are doing. Get away from that coat of yours, Bat, or I'll put a bullet in your stomach."

He had braced himself against the door in anticipation of the thrust of the man, but it seemed as though the prisoner inside had accepted the situation, for he made no sign.

"So you are all wondering how I knew about the cupboard," he jeered. He held up the gloved hand, and in the palm something flashed back the light of the lamp. Connor knew. The tiny mirror sewn in the palm of the sharper's glove was recognized equipment.

"Now, gentlemen," said Jimmy with a mocking laugh, "I must insist on having my way. Connor, you will please bring to me the lady you abducted this afternoon."

Connor hesitated; then he intercepted a glance from Bat Sands, and sullenly withdrew from the room. Jimmy did not speak till Connor had returned ushering in the white-faced girl. He saw that she looked faint and ill, and motioned one of the men to place a chair for her.

What she saw amidst that forbidding group was a young man with a little Vandyke beard, who looked at her with grave, thoughtful eyes. He was a gentleman, she could see that, and her heart leapt within her as she realized that the presence of this man in the fashionably-cut clothes and the most unfashionable pistol meant deliverance from this horrible place.

"Miss Kent," he said kindly.

She nodded, she could not trust herself to speak. The experience of the past few hours had almost reduced her to a state of collapse. Jimmy saw the girl was on the verge of a breakdown.

"I am going to take you home," he said, and added whimsically, "and cannot but feel that you have underrated your opportunities. Not often will you see gathered together so splendid a collection of our profession."

He waved his hand in introduction. "Bat Sands, Miss Kent, a most lowly thief, possibly worse. George Collroy, coiner and a ferocious villain. Vinnis, who follows the lowest of all grades of dishonest livelihood—blackmailer. Here," Jimmy went on, as he stepped aside from the cupboard, "is the gem of the collection. I will show you our friend who has so coyly effaced himself."

He addressed the occupant of the cupboard.

"Come out, Goyle," he said sharply. There was no response. Jimmy pointed to one of the ruffians in the—room. "Open that door," he commanded. The man slunk forward and pulled the door open.

"Come out, Goyle," he growled, then stepped back with blank astonishment stamped upon his face. "Why—why," he gasped, "there's nobody there!"

With a cry, Jimmy started forward. One glance convinced him that the man spoke the truth, and then—

There were keen wits in that crowd, men used to crises and quick to act. Bat Sands saw Jimmy's attention diverted for a moment, and Jimmy's pistol hand momentarily lowered.

To think with Bat Sands was to act.

Jimmy, turning back upon the "Lot," saw the life preserver descending, and leapt on one side; then, as he recovered, somebody threw a coat at the lamp, and the room was in darkness.

Jimmy reached out his hand and caught the girl by the arm.

"Into that cupboard," he whispered, pushing her into the recess from which Goyle had so mysteriously vanished. Then, with one hand on the edge of the door, he groped around with his pistol for his assailants. He could hear their breathing and the creak of the floorboards as they came toward him.

He crouched down by the door, judging that the "cosh" would he aimed in a line with his head. By and by he heard the swish of the descending stick, and "crash!" the preserver struck the wall above him.

He was confronted with a difficulty; to fire would be to invite trouble. He had no desire to attract the attention of the police for many reasons. Unless the life of the girl was in danger he resolved to hold his fire, and when Ike Josephs, feeling cautiously forward with his stick, blundered into Jimmy, Ike suddenly dropped to the floor without a cry, because he had been hit a fairly vicious blow in that portion of the anatomy which is dignified with the title "solar plexus."

It was just after this that he heard a startled little cry from the girl behind him, and then a voice that sent his heart into his mouth. "All right! All right! All right!"

There was only one man who used that tag, and Jimmy's heart rose up to bless his name in thankfulness.

"This way, Miss Kent," said the voice, "mind the little step. Don't be afraid of the gentleman on the floor, he's handcuffed and strapped and gagged, and is perfectly harmless."

Jimmy chuckled. The mystery of Angel's intimate knowledge of the "Lot's" plans and of Connor's movements, the disappearance of Goyle, were all explained.

He did not know for certain that the occupant of the "empty" house next door had industriously cut through the thin party-walls that separated the two houses, and had rigged up a "back" to the cupboard that was really a door, but he guessed it.

Then a blinding ray of light shot into the room where the "Borough Lot" still groped for its enemy, and a gentle voice said: "Gentlemen, you may make your choice which way you go—out by the front door, where my friend, Inspector Collyer, with quite large number of men, is waiting; or by the back door, where Sergeant Murtle and exactly seven plain-clothes men are impatiently expecting you."

Bat recognized the voice. "Angel Esquire!" he cried in consternation. From the darkness behind the dazzling electric lamp that threw a narrow lane of light into the apartment came an amused chuckle.

"What is it," asked Angel's persuasive voice, "a cop?"

"It's a fair cop," said Bat truthfully.

V. — THE CRYPTOGRAM

MR. SPEDDING looked at his watch. He stood upon the marble-tiled floor of the Great Deposit. High above his head, suspended from the beautiful dome, blazed a hundred lights from an ornate electrolier. He paced before the great pedestal that towered up from the centre of the building, and the floor was crisscrossed with the shadows of the steel framework that encased it. But for the dozen chairs that were placed in a semicircle before the great granite base, the big hall was bare and unfurnished.

Mr. Spedding walked up and down, and his footsteps rang hollow; when he spoke the misty space of the building caught up his voice and sent down droning echoes.

"There is only the lady to come," he said, looking at his watch again. He spoke to the two men who sat at either extreme of the crescent of chairs.

The one was Jimmy, a brooding, thoughtful figure; the other was Connor, ill at ease and subdued. Behind the chairs, at some distance, stood two men who looked like artisans, as indeed they were: at their feet lay a bag of tools, and on a small board a heap that looked like sand.

At the door a stolid-looking commissionaire waited, his breast glittering with medals.

Footsteps sounded in the vestibule, the rustle of a woman's dress, and Kathleen Kent entered, closely followed by Angel Esquire.

At him the lawyer looked questioningly as he walked forward to greet the girl.

"Mr. Angel has kindly offered me his help," she said timidly—then, recognizing Connor, her face flushed—"and if necessary, his protection."

Mr. Spedding bowed. "I hope you will not find this part of the ceremony trying," he said in a low voice, and led the girl to a chair. Then he made a signal to the commissionaire.

"What is going to happen?" Kathleen whispered to her companion, and Angel shook his head.

"I can only guess," he replied in the same tone. He was looking up at the great safe wherein he knew was stored the wealth of the dead gambler, and wondering at the freakish ingenuity that planned and foresaw this strange scene.

The creak of footsteps in the doorway made him turn his head. He saw a white-robed figure, and behind him a black-coated man in attendance, holding on a cushion a golden casket.

Then the dread, familiar words brought him to his feet with a shiver:—"I am the resurrection and the life, saith the Lord; he that believeth in me, though he were dead, yet shall he live: and whosoever liveth and liveth in me shall never die." The clergyman's solemn voice resounded through the building, and the detective realized that the ashes of the dead man were coming to their last abiding-place.

The slow procession moved toward the silent party. Slowly it paced toward the column; then, as the clergyman's feet rang on the steel stairway that wound upward, he began the Psalm which of all others perhaps most fitted the passing of old Reale:—"Have mercy upon me, O God, after Thy great goodness... Wash me throughly from my wickedness: and cleanse me from my sin... Behold, I was shapen in wickedness... Deliver me from bloodguiltiness, O God... " Halfway up the column a small gap yawned in the unbroken granite face, and into this the golden cabinet was pushed; then the workman, who had formed one of the little party that wound upward, lifted a smooth cube of polished granite.

"Forasmuch as it hath pleased Almighty God of His great mercy to take unto Himself the soul of our dear brother here departed... " The mason's trowel grated on the edges of the cavity, the block of stone was thrust in until it was flush with the surface of the pedestal. Carved on the end of the stone were four words:—

Pulvis Cinis et Nihil.

It was when the workmen had been dismissed, and the lawyer was at the door bidding adieu to the priest whose strange duty had been performed, that Angel crossed to where Jimmy sat. He caught Jimmy's grim smile, and raised his eyes to where all that was mortal of Reale had been placed.

"The Latin?" asked Angel.

"Surprising, isn't it?" said the other quietly. "Reale had seen things, you know. A man who travels picks up information." He nodded toward the epitaph.

"He got that idea at Toledo, in the cathedral there. Do you know it? A slab of brass over a dead king-maker, Portocarrero, 'Hic iacet pulvis cinis et nihil'. I translated it for him; the conceit pleased him. Sitting here, watching his strange funeral, I wondered if 'pulvis cinis et nihil' would come into it."

And now Spedding came creaking back. The workmen had disappeared, the outer door was closed, and the commissionaire had retired to his room leading from the vestibule. In Spedding's hand was a bundle of papers. He took his place with his back to the granite pedestal and lost no time in preliminaries.

"I have here the will of the late James Ryan Reale," he began. "The contents of this will are known to every person here except Miss Kent."

He had a dry humour of his own, this lawyer, as his next words proved.

"A week ago a very clever burglary was committed in my office; the safe was opened, a private dispatch box forced, and my papers ransacked. I must do my visitor justice"—he bowed slightly, first in the direction of Connor, then toward Jimmy—"and say that nothing was taken and practically nothing disturbed. There was plenty of evidence that the object of the burglary was to secure a sight of this will."

Jimmy was unperturbed at the scarcely-veiled charge, and if he moved it was only with the object of taking up an easier position in the chair. Not even the shocked eyes of the girl that looked appealingly toward him caused him any apparent uneasiness.

"Go on," he said, as the lawyer paused as though waiting for an admission. He was quietly amused. He knew very well now who this considerate burglar was.

"By copying this will the burglar or burglars obtained an unfair advantage over the other legatee or legatees." The stiff paper crackled noisily as he unfolded the document in his hand. "I will formally read the will and afterwards explain it to such of you as need the explanation," Spedding resumed. The girl listened as the lawyer began to read. Confused by the legal terminology, the endless repetitions, and the chaotic verbiage of the instrument, she yet realized as the reading went on that this last will and testament of old Reale was something extraordinary. There was mention of houses and estates, freeholds and bonds...

"... and all the residue of any property whatsoever and wheresoever absolutely" that went to somebody. To whom she could not gather. Once she thought it was to herself, "to Francis Corydon Kent, Esquire, or the heirs of his body;" once it sounded as though this huge fortune was to be inherited by "James Cavendish Fairfax Stannard, Baronet of the United Kingdom."

She wondered if this was Jimmy, and remembered in a vague way that she had heard that the ninth baronet of that name was a person of questionable character.

Then again it seemed as if the legatee was to be "Patrick George Connor."

There was a doggerel verse in the will that the lawyer gabbled through, and something about the great safe, then the lawyer came to an end.

In the conventional declaration of the witnesses lay a sting that sent a dull red flush to Connor's cheek and again provoked Jimmy's grim smile. The lawyer read:—"Signed by the above James Ryan Reale as his last will and testament (the word 'thief' after 'James Cavendish Fairfax Stannard, Baronet of the United Kingdom' and the word 'thief' after 'Patrick George Connor,' in the twentieth and twenty-third lines from the top hereof, having been deleted), in the presence of us... "

The lawyer folded the will perversely and put it in his pocket. Then he took four slips of paper from an envelope. "It is quite clear to you gentlemen."

He did not wait for the men's reply, but went on addressing the bewildered girl.

"To you, Miss Kent, I am afraid the will is not so clear. I will explain it in a few words. My late client was the owner of a gambling establishment. Thus he amassed a huge fortune, which he has left to form, if I may so put it, a large prize fund. The competitors are yourselves. Frankly, it is a competition between the dupes, or the heirs of the dupes, who were ruined by my late client, and the men who helped in the fleecing."

The lawyer spoke dispassionately, as though expounding some hypothesis, but there was that in his tone which made Connor wince.

"Your father, my dear young lady, was one of these dupes many years ago—you must have been at school at the time. He became suddenly a poor man."

The girl's face grew hard.

"So that was how it happened," she said slowly.

"That is how it happened," the lawyer repeated gravely. "Your father's fortune was one of four great fortunes that went into the coffers of my late client."

The formal description of Reale seemed to lend him an air of respectability.

"The other three have long since died, neither of them leaving issue. You are the sole representative of the victims. These gentlemen are—let use say—in opposition. This safe," he waved his hand toward the great steel room that crowned the granite column, "contains the fortune. The safe itself is the invention of my late client. Where the lock should be are six dials, on each of which are the letters of the alphabet. The dials are ranged one inside the other, and on one side is a steel pointer. A word of six letters opens the safe. By turning the dials so that the letters come opposite the pointer, and form this word, the door is opened."

He stopped to wipe his forehead, for in the energy of his explanation he had become hot.

Then he resumed—"What that word is, is for you to discover. My late client, who had a passion for acrostics I and puzzles and inventions of every kind, has left a doggerel verse which he most earnestly assured me contained the solution."

He handed a slip first to the girl and then to the others.

For a moment the world swam before Kathleen's eyes.

All that hinged upon that little verse came home to her.

Carefully conning each word, as if in fear of its significance escaping her, she read:—

"Here's a puzzle in language old, Find my meaning and get my gold. Take one Bolt—just one, no more—Fix it on behind a Door. Place it at a river's Mouth East or west or north or south. Take some Leaves and put them whole In some water in a Bowl. I found this puzzle in a book From which some mighty truths were took."

She read again and yet again, the others watching her. With every reading she seemed to get further from the solution of the mystery, and she turned in despair to Angel.

"I can make nothing of it," she cried helplessly, "nothing, nothing, nothing."

41

"It is, with due respect to my late client, the veriest doggerel," said the lawyer frankly, "and yet on that the inheritance of the whole of his fortune depends."

He had noticed that neither Connor nor Jimmy had read the slips he had handed to them.

"The paper I have given you is a facsimile reproduction of the original copy, and that may be inspected at any time at my office."

The girl was scanning the rhyme in an agony of perplexity. "Ishall never do it," she said in despair.

Angel took the paper gently from her hand. "Don't attempt it," he said kindly. "There is plenty of time. I do not think that either of your rival competitors have gained anything by the advantage they have secured. I also have had in my possession a copy of the rhyme for the past week."

The girl's eyes opened wide in astonishment. "You?" she said.

Angel's explanation was arrested by a singular occurrence.

Connor sat at one end of the row of chairs moodily eying the paper.

Jimmy thoughtfully stroking his beard at the other end, suddenly rose and walked to where his brooding confederate sat. The man shrunk back as he approached, and Jimmy, seating himself by his side, bent forward and said something in a low voice. He spoke rapidly, and Angel, watching them closely, saw a look of incredulous surprise come into Connor's face. Then wrath and incredulity mingled, and Connor sprang up, striking the back of the chair with his fist.

"What?" he roared. "Give up a chance of a fortune? I'll see you—"

Jimmy's voice never rose, but he gripped Connor's arm and pulled him down into his chair.

"I won't! I won't! D'ye think I'm going to throw away—"

Jimmy released the man's arm and rose with a shrug of his shoulders. He walked to where Kathleen was standing.

"Miss Kent," he said, and hesitated. "It is difficult for me to say what I have to say; but I want to tell you that so far as I am concerned the fortune is yours. I shall make no claim to it, and I will afford you every assistance that lies in my power to discover the word that is hidden in the verse."

The girl made no reply. Her lips were set tight, and the hard look that Angel had noticed when the lawyer had referred to her father came back again.

Jimmy waited a moment for her to speak, but she made no sign, and with a slight bow he walked toward the door. "Stop!" It was Kathleen that spoke, and Jimmy turned and waited.

"As I understand this will," she said slowly, "you are one of the men to whom my father owed his ruin."

His eyes met hers unfalteringly. "Yes," he said simply.

"One of the men that I have to thank for years of misery and sorrow," she continued. "When I saw my father slowly sinking, a broken-hearted man, weighed down with the knowledge of the folly that had brought his wife and child to comparative poverty; when I saw my father die, crushed in spirit by his misfortunes, I never thought I should meet the man who brought his ruin about."

Still Jimmy's gaze did not waver. Impassive, calm and imperturbable, he listened unmoved to the bitter indictment.

"This will says you were a man of my father's own class, one who knew the tricks by which a gentle, simple man, with a childish faith in such men as you, might be lured into temptation."

Jimmy made no reply, and the girl went on in biting tones—"A few days ago you helped me to escape from men whom you introduced with an air of superiority as thieves and blackmailers. That it was you who rendered me this service I shall regret to the end of my days. You! You! You!"

She flung out her hand scornfully. "If they were thieves, what are you? A gambler's tout? A decoy? A harpy preying on the weakness of your unfortunate fellows?"

She turned to Connor. "Had this man offered me his help I might have accepted it. Had he offered to forego his claim to this fortune I might have been impressed by his generosity. From you, whom God gave advantages of birth and education, and who utilized them to bring ruin and disaster on such men as my father, the offer is an insult!"

Jimmy's face was deadly pale, but he made no sign. Only his eyes shone brighter, and the hand that twisted the point of his beard twitched nervously.

The girl turned to Angel wearily. Her outburst and the tension of the evening had exhausted her. "Will you take me home, Mr. Angel?" she said. She offered her hand to the lawyer, who had been an interested observer of the scene, and ignoring the two men, she turned to go.

Then Jimmy spoke. "I do not attempt to excuse myself, Miss Kent," he said evenly; "for my life and my acts I am unaccountable to man or woman. Your condemnation makes it neither easier nor harder to live my life. Your charity might have made a difference."

He held out a detaining hand, for Kathleen had gathered up her skirts to move away. "I have considered your question fairly. I am one of the men to whom your father owed his ruin, insomuch as I was one of Reale's associates. I am not one of the men, insomuch as I used my every endeavour to dissuade your father from taking the risks he took."

The humour of some recollection took hold of him, and a grim little smile came into his face. "You say I betrayed your father," he said in the same quiet tone. "As a fact I betrayed Reale. I was at trouble to explain to your father the secret of Reale's electric roulette table; I demonstrated the futility of risking another farthing." He laughed. "I have said I would not excuse myself, and here I am pleading like a small boy, 'If you please, it wasn't me,'" he said a little impatiently; and then he added abruptly, "I will not detain you," and walked away.

He knew instinctively that she waited a moment hesitating for a reply, then he heard the rustle of her dress and knew she had gone. He stood looking upward to where the graven granite set marked the ashes of Reale, until her footsteps had died away and the lawyer's voice broke the silence.

"Now, Sir James—" he began, and Jimmy spun round with an oath, his face white with passion.

"Jimmy," he said in a harsh voice, "Jimmy is my name, and I want to hear no other, if you please."

Mr. Spedding, used as he was to the wayward phases of men, was a little startled at the effect of his words, and hastened to atone for his blunder. "I—I beg your pardon," he said quickly. "I merely wished to say—"

Jimmy did not wait to hear what he said, but turned upon Connor. "I've got a few words to say to you," he said. His voice had gone back to its calm level, but there was a menace in its quietness. "When I persuaded Angel to give you a chance to get away on the night the 'Borough Lot' was arrested, I hoped I could get you to agree with me that the money should be handed to Miss Kent when the word was found. I knew in my inmost heart that this was a forlorn hope," he went on, "that there is no gold in the quartz of your composition. You are just beast all through."

He paced the floor of the hall for a minute or two, then he stopped.

"Connor," he said suddenly, "you tried to take my life the other night. I have a mind to retaliate. You may go ahead and puzzle out the word that unlocks that safe. Get it by any means that suggest themselves to you. Steal it, buy it—do anything you wish. The day you secure the key to Reale's treasure I shall kill you."

He talked like a man propounding a simple business proposition, and the lawyer, who in his early youth had written a heavy little paper on "The Congenital Criminal," listened and watched, and, in quite a respectable way, gloated.

Jimmy picked up his hat and coat from a chair, and nodding to the lawyer, strolled out of the hall. In the vestibule where the one commissionaire had been were six. Every man was a non-commissioned officer, and, as was apparent from his medals, had seen war service. Jimmy noted the belt about each man and the dangling revolver holster, and approved of the lawyer's precaution.

"Night guard, sergeant—major?" he asked, addressing one whose crowned sleeve showed his rank.

"Day and night guard, sir," replied the officer quietly.

"Good," said Jimmy, and passed out into the street. And now only the lawyer and Connor remained, and as Jimmy left, they too prepared for departure. The lawyer was mildly interested in the big, heavy criminal who walked by his side. He was a fairly familiar type of the bull-headed desperado.

"There is nothing I can explain?" asked Spedding, as they stood together in the vestibule. Connor's eyes were on the guard, and he frowned a little.

"You don't trust us very much," he said.

"I don't trust you at all," said the lawyer.

VI. — A THE RED ENVELOPE

MR. SPEDDING, the admirable lawyer, lived on Clapham Common, where he owned the freehold of that desirable residence, "High Holly Lodge." He was a bachelor, with a taste for bridge parties and Madeira. Curious neighbours would have been mystified if they had known that Mr. Spedding's repair bill during the first two years of his residence was something well over three thousand pounds.

What they did know was that Mr. Spedding "had the builders in" for an unconscionable time, that they were men who spoke in a language entirely foreign to Clapham, and that they were housed during the period of renovation in a little galvanized iron bungalow erected for the purpose in the grounds. A neighbour on visiting terms expressed his opinion that for all the workmen had done he could discern no material difference in the structure of the house, and from his point of view the house presented the same appearance after the foreign builders left, as it did before their advent. Mr. Spedding met all carelessly-applied questions concerning the extent of the structural alterations with supreme discretion. He spoke vaguely about a new system of ventilation, and hinted at warmth by radiation.

Suburbia loves to show off its privately conceived improvements to property, but Mr. Spedding met veiled hints of a desire to inspect his work with that comfortable smile which was so valuable an asset of his business.

It was a few evenings after the scene in the Lombard Street Deposit that Mr. Spedding sat in solitude before his modest dinner at Clapham. An evening newspaper lay by the side of his chair, and he picked it up at intervals to read again the paragraph which told of the release of the "Borough Lot."

The paragraph read:—

"The men arrested in connection with the gambling raid at Poplar were discharged today, the police, it is understood, failing to secure sufficient evidence to justify a prosecution."

The lawyer shook his head doubtfully. "I rather like Angel Esquire's definition," he said with a wry smile. "It is a neat method of saving the face of the police, but I could wish that the 'Borough Lot' were out of the way."

Later he had occasion to change his opinion.

A tap at the door preceded the entry of a sedate butler. The lawyer looked at the card on the tray, and hesitated; then, "Show him in," he said.

Jimmy came into the room, and bowed slightly to the elder man, who rose at his entrance. They waited in silence till the servant had closed the door behind him. "To what am I indebted?" began the lawyer, and motioned his visitor to a seat.

"May I smoke?" asked Jimmy, and Mr. Spedding nodded.

"It is in the matter of Reale's millions," said Jimmy, and allowed his eyes to follow the cloud of smoke he blew.

"I thought it was understood that this was a subject which might only be discussed at my office and in business hours?" said the lawyer sharply, and Jimmy nodded again.

"You will confess, Mr. Spedding," he said easily, "that the Reale will is sufficiently unconventional to justify any departure from established custom on the part of the fortunate or unfortunate legatees."

Mr. Spedding made an impatient movement of his hand.

"I do not inquire into your business," Jimmy went on smoothly enough, "and I am wholly incurious as to in what strange manner you became acquainted with your late client, or what fees you received to undertake so extraordinary a commission; but I am satisfied that you are recompensed for such trifling inconveniences as—say—an after-dinner visit from myself."

Jimmy had a way of choosing his words, hesitating for the exact expression that would best convey every shade of his meaning. The lawyer, too, recognized the logic of the speech, and contented himself with a shrug which meant nothing.

"I do not inquire into your motives," Jimmy resumed; "it pleases me to believe that they are entirely disinterested, that your attitude is the ideal one as between client and agent."

His pause was longer this time, and the lawyer was piqued into interjecting an impatient—"Well?"

"Well," said Jimmy slowly, "believing all this, let us say, I am at a loss to know why at the reading of the will you gave us no indication of the existence of a key to this mysterious verse."

"There is no key," said the lawyer quickly, and added, "so far as I know."

"That you did not tell us," Jimmy went on, as though unconscious of any interruption, "of the big red envelope—"

Spedding sprang to his feet white as death. "The envelope," he stammered angrily, "what do you know—what envelope?"

Jimmy's hand waved him to his seat. "Let us have no emotions, no flights, no outraged honour, I beg of you, dear Mr. Spedding. I do not suggest that you have any sinister reasons for withholding information concerning what my friend Angel would call the 'surprise packet'. In good time I do not doubt you would have disclosed its existence."

"I know of no red envelope," said the lawyer doggedly.

"I rather fancied you would say that," said Jimmy, with a touch of admiration in his tone. "You are not the sort of fox to curl up and howl at the first bay of the hound—if you will permit the simile—indeed, you would have disappointed me if you had."

The lawyer paced the room. "Look here," he said, coming to a halt before the semi-recumbent form that lay behind a haze of cigarette smoke in the arm-chair, "you've spent a great deal of your time telling me what I am, describing my many doubtful qualities, and hinting more or less broadly that I am a fairly representative scoundrel. May I ask what is is your ultimate object? Is it blackmail?" he demanded harshly.

"No," said Jimmy, by no means disconcerted by the brutality of the question. "Are you begging, or borrowing, or—"

"Stealing?" murmured Jimmy lazily.

"All that I have to say to you is, finish your business and go. Furthermore, you are at liberty to come with me tomorrow morning and search my office and question my clerks. I will accompany you to my banks, and to the strong-room I rent at the deposit. Search for this red envelope you speak about, and if you find it, you are at liberty to draw the worst deductions you will."

Jimmy pulled gently at his cigarette with reflective eyes cast upward to the ceiling. "Do you speak Spanish?" he asked.

"No," said the other impatiently.

"It's a pity," said Jimmy, with a note of genuine regret. "Spanish is a very useful language—especially in the Argentine, for which delightful country, I understand, lawyers who betray their trust have an especial predilection. My Spanish needs a little furbishing, and only the other day I was practising with a man whose name, I believe, is Murrello. Do you know him?"

"If you have completed your business, I will ring for the servant," said the lawyer.

"He told me—my Spaniard, I mean—a curious story. He comes from Barcelona, and by way of being a mason or something of the sort, was brought to England with some other of his fellow-countrymen to make some curious alterations to the house of a Senor in—er—Clapham of all places in the world."

The lawyer's breath came short and fast.

"From what I was able to gather," Jimmy went on languidly, "and my Spanish is Andalusian rather than Catalonian, so that I missed some of his interesting narrative, these alterations partook of the nature of wonderfully concealed strong-rooms—steel doors artfully covered with cheap wood carving, vaults cunningly constructed beneath innocent basement kitchens, little stairways in apparently solid walls and the like."

The levity went out of his voice, and he straightened himself in his chair.

"I have no desire to search your office," he said quietly, "or perhaps I should say no further desire, for I have already methodically examined every hole and corner. No," he checked the words on Spedding's lips, "no, it was not I who committed the blundering burglary you spoke of. You never found traces of me, I'll swear. You may keep the keys of your strong-room, and I shall not trouble your bankers."

"What do you want?" demanded the lawyer shortly.

"I want to see what you have got downstairs," was the reply, and there was no doubting its earnestness, "and more especially do I want to see the red envelope."

The lawyer bent his brows in thought. His eyes were fixed unwaveringly on Jimmy's. "Suppose," he said slowly, "suppose that such an envelope did exist, suppose for the sake of argument these mysterious vaults and secret chambers are, as you suggest, in existence, what right have you, more than any other one of the beneficiaries under the will, to demand a private examination? Why should I give you an unfair advantage over them?"

Jimmy rose to his feet and stretched himself before replying. "There is only one legatee whom I recognize," he said briefly, "that is the girl. The money is hers. I do not want a farthing. I am equally determined that nobody else shall touch a penny—neither my young friend Connor "—he stopped to give emphasis to the next two words—"nor yourself."

"Sir!" said the outraged Mr. Spedding.

"Nor yourself, Mr. Spedding," repeated Jimmy with conviction. "Let us understand each other thoroughly. You are, as I read you, a fairly respectable citizen. I would trust you with ten or a hundred thousand pounds without experiencing the slightest anxiety. I would not trust you with two millions in solid cash, nor would I trust any man. The magnitude of the sum is calculated to overwhelm your moral sense. The sooner the red envelope is in the possession of Angel Esquire the better for us all."

Spedding stood with bent head, his fingers nervously stroking his jaw, thinking.

"An agile mind this," thought Jimmy; "if I am not careful there will be trouble here." He watched the lawyer's face, and noticed the lines suddenly disappear from the troubled face, and the placid smile returning. "Conciliation and partial confession," judged Jimmy, and his diagnosis was correct.

"Well, Mr. Jimmy," said Spedding, with some show of heartiness, "since you know so much, it may be as well to tell you more. As you have so cleverly discovered, my house to a great extent is a strong-room. There are many valuable documents that I could not with any confidence leave deposited at my office. They are safer here under my eye, so to speak. The papers of the late Mr. Reale are, I confess, in this house; but—now mark me—whether the red envelope you speak of is amongst these I do not know. There is a multitude of documents in connection with the case, all of which I have had no time to go through. The hour is late, but—" He paused irresolutely. "—If you would care to inspect the mysteries of the basement "—he smiled benevolently, and was his old self—"I shall be happy to have your assistance in a cursory search."

Jimmy was alert and watchful and to the point. "Lead the way," he said shortly, and Spedding, after a moment's hesitation, opened the door and Jimmy followed him into the hall.

Contrary to his expectations, the lawyer led him upstairs, and through a plainly furnished bedroom to a small dressing room that opened off. There was a conventional wardrobe against the wall, and this Spedding opened. A dozen suits hung from hooks and stretchers, and the lawyer groped amongst these for a moment. Then there was a soft click, and the back of the wardrobe swung back. Spedding turned to his visitor with a quizzical smile.

"Your friend Angel's method of gaining admittance to the haunt of the 'Borough Lot' was not original. Come."

Jimmy stepped gingerly through into the darkness. He heard the snap of a button, and a soft glow of light revealed a tiny chamber, in which two men might comfortably stand upright. The back of the wardrobe closed, and they were alone in a little room about as large as an average cupboard. There was a steel lever on one side of the walls, and this the lawyer pulled cautiously. Jimmy felt a sinking sensation, and heard a faint, far-off buzzing of machinery.

"An electric lift, I take it," he said quietly.

"An electric lift," repeated the lawyer.

Down, down, down they sank, till Jimmy calculated that they must be at least twenty feet below the street level. Then the lift slowed down and stopped at a door. Spedding opened this with a key he took from his pocket, and they stepped out into a chill, earthy darkness.

"There's a light here," said the lawyer, and groped for the switch. They were in a large vaulted apartment lit from the roof. At one end a steel door faced them, and ranged about the vault on iron racks a number of black japanned boxes.

Jimmy noted the inscriptions, and was a little surprised at the extent and importance of the solicitor's practice. Spedding must have read his thoughts, for he turned with a smile.

"Not particularly suggestive of a defaulting solicitor," he said ironically.

"Two million pounds," replied Jimmy immediately, "that is my answer to you, Mr. Spedding. An enormous fortune for the reaching. I wouldn't trust the Governors of the Bank of England."

Spedding may have been annoyed as he walked to the door in the wall and opened it, but he effectively concealed his annoyance. As the door fell backward, Jimmy saw a little apartment, four feet by six feet, with a roof he could touch with his hand. There was a fresh current of air, but from whence it came he could not discover. The only articles of furniture in the little cell were a writing table and a swing chair placed exactly beneath the electric lamp in the roof. Spedding pulled open a drawer in the desk.

"I do not keep my desks locked here," he said pleasantly enough. It was characteristic of him that he indulged in no preamble, no apologetic preliminaries, and that he showed no sign of embarrassment as he slipped his hand into the drawer, and drawing forth a bulky red envelope, threw it on to the desk. You might have forgotten that his last words were denials that the red envelope had existed.

Jimmy looked at him curiously, and the lawyer returned his gaze.

"A new type?" he asked.

"Hardly," said Jimmy cheerfully. "I once knew a man like you in the Argentine—he was hanged eventually."

"Curious," mused the lawyer, "I have often thought I might be hanged, but have never quite seen why—" He nearly added something else, but checked himself.

Jimmy had the red envelope in his hand and was examining it closely. It was heavily sealed with the lawyer's own seal, and bore the inscription in Reale's crabbed, illiterate handwriting, "Puzzle Ideas."

He weighed it and pinched it. There was a little compact packet inside.

"I shall open this," said Jimmy decisively. "You, of course, have already examined it."

The lawyer made no reply. Jimmy broke the seal of the envelope. Half his mind was busy in speculation as to its contents, the other half was engaged with the lawyer's plans. Jimmy was too experienced a man to be deceived by the complaisance of the smooth Mr. Spedding. He watched his every move. All the while he was engaged in what appeared to be a concentrated examination of the packet his eyes never left the lawyer. That Spedding made no sign was a further proof in Jimmy's eyes that the coup was to come.

"We might as well examine the envelope upstairs as here," said the lawyer. The other man nodded, and followed him from the cell. Spedding closed the steel door and locked it, then turned to Jimmy.

"Do you notice," he said with some satisfaction, "how skilfully this chamber is constructed?" He waved his hand round the larger vault, at the iron racks and the shiny black boxes.

Jimmy was alert now. The lawyer's geniality was too gratuitous, his remarks a trifle inapropos. It was like the lame introduction to a story which the teller was anxious to drag in at all hazards.

"Here, for instance," said the lawyer, tapping one of the boxes, "is what appears to be an ordinary deed box. As a matter of fact, it is an ingenious device for trapping burglars, if they should by any chance reach the vault. It is not opened by an ordinary key, but by the pressure of a button, either in my room or here."

He walked leisurely to the end of the vault, Jimmy following.

For a man of his build Spedding was a remarkably agile man. Jimmy had underrated his agility. He realized this when suddenly the lights went out. Jimmy sprang for the lawyer, and struck the rough stone wall of the vault. He groped quickly left and right, and grasped only the air.

"Keep quiet," commanded Spedding's calm voice from the other end of the chamber, "and keep cool. I am going to show you my burglar catcher."

Jimmy's lingers were feeling along the wall for the switch that controlled the lights. As if divining his intention, the lawyer's voice said—" The lights are out of control, Jimmy, and I am fairly well out of your reach."

"We shall see," was Jimmy's even reply.

"And if you start shooting you will only make the atmosphere of this place a little more unbreathable than it is at present," Spedding went on.

Jimmy smiled in the darkness, and the lawyer heard the snap of a Colt pistol as his captive loaded.

"Did you notice the little ventilator?" asked the lawyer's voice again. "Well, I am behind that. Between my unworthy body and your nickel bullets there are two feet of solid masonry."

Jimmy made no reply, his pistol went back to his hip again. He had his electric lamp in his pocket, but prudently kept it there. "Before we go any further," he said slowly, "will you be good enough to inform me as to your intentions?"

He wanted three minutes, he wanted them very badly; perhaps two minutes would be enough. All the time the lawyer was speaking he was actively employed. He had kicked off his shoes when the lights went out, and now he stole round the room, his sensitive hands flying over the stony walls.

"As to my intentions," the lawyer was saying, "it must be fairly obvious to you that I am not going to hand you over to the police. Rather, my young friend, in the vulgar parlance of the criminal classes, I am going to 'do you in', meaning thereby, if you will forgive the legal terminology, that I shall assist you to another and, I hope, though I am not sanguine, a better world."

He heard Jimmy's insolent laugh in the blackness.

"You are a man after my own heart, Jimmy," he went on regretfully. "I could have wished that I might have been spared this painful duty; but it is a duty, one that I owe to society and myself."

"You are an amusing person," said Jimmy's voice.

"I am glad you think so. Jimmy, my young friend, I am afraid our conversation must end here. Do you know anything of chemistry?"

"A little."

"Then you will appreciate my burglar catcher," said Spedding, with uncanny satisfaction. "You, perhaps, noticed the japanned box with the perforated lid? You did? Good! There are two compartments, and two chemicals in certain quantities kept apart. My hand is on the key now that will combine them. When cyanide of potassium is combined with sulphuric acid, do you know what gas is formed?"

Jimmy did not reply. He had found what he had been searching for. His talk with the Spanish builder had been to some purpose. It was a little stony projection from the wall. He pressed it downward, and was sensible of a sensation of coldness. He reached out his hand, and found where solid wall had been a blank space.

"Do you hear, Jimmy?" asked the lawyer's voice.

"I hear," replied Jimmy, and felt for the edge of the secret door. His fingers sliding down the smooth surface of the flange encountered the two catches.

"It is hydrocyanic acid," said the lawyer's smooth voice, and Jimmy heard the snap of the button. "Goodbye," said the lawyer's voice again, and Jimmy reeled back through the open doorway swinging the door behind him, and carrying with him a whiff of air heavily laden with the scent of almonds.

VII. — WHAT THE RED ENVELOPE HELD

"MY dear Angel," wrote Jimmy, "I commend to you one Mr. Spedding, an ingenious man. If by chance you ever wish to visit him, do so in business hours. If you desire to examine his most secret possession, effect an entrance into a dreary-looking house at the corner of Cley's Road, a stone's-throw from 'High Holly Lodge'. It is marked in plain characters 'To Let,' In the basement you will find a coal-cellar. Searching the coal-cellar diligently, you will discover a flight of stone steps leading to a subterranean passage, which burrows under the ground until it arrives at friend Spedding's particular private vault. If this reads like a leaf torn from Dumas or dear Harrison Ainsworth it is not my fault. I visited our legal adviser last night, and had quite a thrilling evening. That I am alive this morning is a tribute to my caution and foreseeing wisdom. The result of my visit is this: I have the key of the 'safe-word' in my hands. Come and get it."

Angel found the message awaiting him when he reached Scotland Yard that morning. He too had spent sleepless hours in a futile attempt to unravel the mystery of old Reale's doggerel verse.

A telegram brought Kathleen Kent to town. Angel met her at a quiet restaurant in Rupert Street, and was struck by the delicate beauty of this slim girl with the calm, gray eyes. She greeted him with a sad little smile.

"I was afraid you would never see me again after my outburst of the other night," she said. "This—this—person is a friend of yours?"

"Jimmy?" asked the detective cheerily. "Oh, yes, Jimmy's by way of being a friend; but he deserved all you said, and he knows it, Miss Kent."

The girl's face darkened momentarily as she thought of Jimmy. "I shall never understand," she said slowly, "how a man of his gifts allowed himself to become—"

"But," protested the detective, "he told you he took no part in the decoying of your father."

The girl turned with open-eyed astonishment. "Surely you do not expect me to believe his excuses," she cried.

Angel Esquire looked grave. "That is just what I should ask you to believe," he said quietly. "Jimmy makes no excuses, and he would certainly tell no lie in extenuation of his faults."

"But—but," said Kathleen, bewildered, "he is a thief by his own showing—a bad man."

"A thief," said Angel soberly, "but not a bad man. Jimmy is a puzzle to most people. To me he is perfectly understandable; that is because I have too much of the criminal in my own composition, perhaps."

"I wish, oh, how I wish I had your faith in him! Then I could absolve him from suspicion of having helped ruin my poor father."

"I think you can do that," said the detective almost eagerly. "Believe me, Jimmy is not to be judged by conventional standards. If you ask me to describe him, I would say that he is a genius who works in an eccentric circle that sometimes overlaps, sometimes underreaches the rigid circle of the law. If you asked me as a policeman, and if I was his bitterest enemy, what I could do with Jimmy, I should say, 'Nothing'. I know of no crime with which I could charge him, save at times with associating with doubtful characters. As a matter of fact, that equally applies to me. Listen, Miss Kent. The first big international case I figured in was a gigantic fraud on the Egyptian Bank. Some four hundred thousand pounds were involved, and whilst from the outsider's point of view Jimmy was beyond suspicion, yet we who were working at the case suspected him, and pretty strongly. The men who owned the bank were rich Egyptians, and the head of all was a Somebody-or-other-Pasha, as great a scoundrel as ever drew breath. It is impossible to tell a lady exactly how big a scoundrel he was, but you may guess. Well, the Pasha knew it was Jimmy who had done the trick, and we knew, but we dare not say so. The arrest of Jimmy would have automatically ruined the banker. That was where I realized the kind of man I had to deal with, and I am always prepared when Jimmy's name is mentioned in connection with a big crime to discover that his victim deserved all he got, and a little more."

The girl gave a little shiver. "It sounds dreadful. Cannot such a man as that employ his talents to a greater advantage?"

Angel shrugged his shoulders despairingly. "I've given up worrying about misapplied talents; it is a subject that touches me too closely," he said. "But as to Jimmy, I'm rather glad you started the conversation in that direction, because I'm going to ask you to meet him today."

"Oh, but I couldn't," she began.

"You are thinking of what happened on the night the will was read? Well, you must forget that. Jimmy has the key to the verse, and it is absolutely imperative that you should be present this afternoon."

With some demur, she consented. In the sitting-room of Jimmy's flat the three sat round a table littered with odds and ends of papers. The girl had met him with some trepidation, and his distant bow had done more to assure her than had he displayed a desire to rehabilitate himself in her good opinion.

Without any preliminaries, Jimmy showed the contents of the packet. He did not explain to the girl by what means he had come into possession of them.

"Of all these papers," began Jimmy, tapping the letter before him, "only one is of any service, and even that makes confusion worse confounded. Reale had evidently had this cursed cryptogram in his mind for a long time. He had made many experiments, and rejected many. Here is one."

He pushed over a card, which bore a few words in Reale's characteristic hand. Angel read:—

"The word of five letters I will use, namely: 1. White every 24 sec. 2. Fixed white and red. 3. White group two every 30 sec. 4. Group occ. white red sec. 30 sec. 5. Fixed white and red."

Underneath was written:

"No good; too easy."

The detective's brows were bent in perplexity. "I'm blessed if I can see where the easiness comes in," he said. "To me it seems so much gibberish, and as difficult as the other."

Jimmy noted the detective's bewilderment with a quiet smile of satisfaction. He did not look directly at the girl, but out of the corner of his eyes he could see her eager young face bent over the card, her pretty forehead wrinkled in a despairing attempt to decipher the curious document.

"Yet it was easy," he said, "and if Reale had stuck to that word, the safe would have been opened by now."

Angel pored over the mysterious clue. "The word, as far as I can gather," said Jimmy, "is 'smock,' but it may be—"

"How on earth—" began Angel in amazement.

"Oh, it's easy," said Jimmy cheerfully, "and I am surprised that an old traveller like yourself should have missed it."

"Group occ. white red sec. 30 sec.," read Angel.

Jimmy laughed.

It was the first time the girl had seen this strange man throw aside his habitual restraint, and she noted with an unaccountable satisfaction that he was decidedly handsome when amused.

"Let me translate it for you," said Jimmy. "Let me expand it into, 'Group occulting White with Red Sectors every Thirty Seconds.' Now do you understand?"

Angel shook his head. "You may think I am shockingly dense," he said frankly, "but even with your lucid explanation I am still in the dark."

Jimmy chuckled. "Suppose you went to Dover tonight, and sat at the end of the Admiralty Pier. It is a beautiful night, with stars in the sky, and you are looking toward France, and you see—?"

"Nothing," said Angel slowly; "a few ships' lights, perhaps, and the flash of the Calais Lighthouse—"

"The occulting flash?" suggested Jimmy.

"The occ.! By Jove!"

"Glad you see it," said Jimmy briskly. "What old Reale did was to take the names of five famous lights—any nautical almanac will give you them: Sanda. Milford Haven. Orkneys. Caldy Island. Kinnaird Head. They form an acrostic, and the initial letters form the work 'smock '; but it was too easy— and too hard, because there are two or three lights, particularly the fixed lights, that are exactly the same, so he dropped that idea."

Angel breathed an admiring sigh. "Jimmy, you're a wonder," he said simply.

Jimmy, busying himself amongst the papers, stole a glance at the girl.

"I am very human," he thought, and was annoyed at the discovery.

"Now we come to the more important clue," he said, and smoothed a crumpled paper on the table. "This, I believe, to have a direct bearing on the verse."

Then three heads came close together over the scrawled sheet.

"A picture of a duck, which means T," spelt Angel, "and that's erased; and then it is a snake that means T—"

Jimmy nodded.

"In Reale's verse," he said deliberately, "there are six words; outside of those six words I am convinced the verse has no meaning. Six words strung together, and each word in capitals. Listen."

He took from his pocketbook the familiar slip on which the verse was written:

"Here's a puzzle in language old, Find my meaning and get my gold. Take one BOLT—just one, no more—Fix it on behind a DOOR. Place it at a river's MOUTH East or west or north or south. Take some LEAVES and put them whole In some WATER in a BOWL. I found this puzzle in a book From which some mighty truths were took."

"There are six words," said Jimmy, and scribbled them down as he spoke:

"Bolt (or Bolts). Leave (or Leaves). Door. Water. Mouth. Bowl. Each one stands for a letter—but what letter?"

"It's rather hopeless if the old man has searched round for all sorts of out-of-the-way objects, and allowed them to stand for letters of the alphabet," said Angel.

The girl murmured something, and met Jimmy's inquiring eyes.

"I was only saying," she said hesitatingly, "that there seems to be a method in all this."

"Except," said Jimmy, "for this," and he pointed to the crossed-out duck.

"By that it would seem that Reale chose his symbols hap-hazard, and that the duck not pleasing him, he substituted the snake."

"But," said Kathleen, addressing Angel, "doesn't it seem strange that an illiterate man like Mr. Reale should make even these rough sketches unless he had a model to draw from?"

"Miss Kent is right," said Jimmy quickly.

"And," she went on, gaining confidence as she spoke, "is there not something about these drawings that reminds you of something?"

"Of what?" asked Angel.

"I cannot tell," she replied, shaking her head; "and yet they remind me of something, and worry me, just as a bar of music that I cannot play worries me. I feel sure that I have seen them before, that they form a part of some system—" She stopped suddenly. "I know," she continued in a lower voice; "they are associated in my mind—with—with the Bible."

The two men stared at her in blank astonishment.

Then Jimmy sprang to his feet, alight with excitement. "Yes, yes," he cried. "Angel, don't you see? The last two lines of Reale's doggerel—

"'I found this puzzle in a book From which some mighty truths were took'"

"Go on, go on, Miss Kent," cried Angel eagerly. "You are on the right track. Try to think—"

Kathleen hesitated, then turned to Jimmy to address the first remark she had directed to him personally that day.

"You haven't got—?"

Jimmy's smile was a little hard. "I'm sorry to disappoint you, Miss Kent, but I have got a copy," he said, with a touch of bitterness in his tone.

He walked to the bookcase at one end of the room and reached down the book—a well-worn volume—and placed it before her.

The rebuke in his voice was deserved, she felt that. She turned the leaves over quickly, but inspiration seemed to have died, for there was nothing in the sacred volume that marshalled her struggling thoughts.

"Is it a text?" asked Angel.

She shook her head. "It is—something," she said. "That sounds vague, doesn't it? I thought if I had the book in my hand, it would recall everything."

Angel was intently studying the rebus. "Here's one letter, anyway. You said that, Jimmy?"

"The door?" said Jimmy. "Yes, that's fairly evident. Whatever the word is, its second letter is 'P'. You see Reale's scribbled notes? All these are no good, the other letters are best, I suppose it means; so we can cut out 'T,' 'O,' and 'K'. The best clue of all," he went on, "is the notes about the 'professor'. You see them:

"Mem: To get the professor's new book on it.

"Mem: To do what the professor thinks right.

"Mem: To write to professor about—'

"Now the questions are: Who is the professor, what is his book, and what did he advise? Reale was in correspondence with him, that is certain; in his desire for accuracy, Reale sought his advice. In all these papers there is no trace of a letter, and if any book exists it is still in Sped—it is still in the place from whence this red envelope came."

The two men exchanged a swift glance.

"Yes," said Angel, as if answering the other's unspoken thought, "it might be done."

The girl looked from one to the other in doubt.

"Does this mean an extra risk?" she asked quietly. "I have not questioned you as to how this red envelope came into your possession, but I have a feeling that it was not obtained without danger."

Angel disregarded Jimmy's warning frown. He was determined that the better side of his strange friend's character should be made evident to the girl.

"Jimmy faced death in a particularly unpleasant form to secure the packet, Miss Kent," he said.

"Then I forbid any further risk," she said spiritedly. "I thought I had made it clear that I would not accept favours at your friend's hands; least of all do I want the favour of his life."

Jimmy heard her unmoved. He had a bitter tongue when he so willed, and he chose that moment. "I do not think you can too strongly impress upon Miss Kent the fact that I am an interested party in this matter," he said acidly. "As she refused my offer to forego my claim to a share of the fortune, she might remember that my interest in the legacy is at least as great as hers. I am risking what I risk, not so much from the beautifully quixotic motives with which she doubtless credits me, as from a natural desire to help myself."

She winced a little at the bluntness of his speech; then recognizing she was in the wrong, she grew angry with herself at her indiscretion.

"If the book is—where these papers were, it can be secured," Jimmy continued, regaining his suavity. "If the professor is still alive he will be found, and by to-morrow I shall have in my possession a list of every book that has ever been written by a professor of anything." Some thought tickled him, and he laughed for the second time that afternoon. "There's a fine course of reading for us all," he said with a little chuckle. "Heaven knows into what mysterious regions the literary professor will lead us. I know one professor who has written a treatise on Sociology that runs into ten volumes, and another who has spoken his mind on Inductive Logic to the extent of twelve hundred closely-printed pages. I have in my mind's eye a vision of three people sitting amidst a chaos of thoughtful literature, searching ponderous tomes for esoteric references to bolts, door, mouth, et cetera."

The picture he drew was too much for the gravity of the girl, and her friendship with the man who was professedly a thief, and by inference something worse, began with a ripple of laughter that greeted his sally.

Jimmy gathered up the papers, and carefully replaced them in the envelope. This he handed to Angel. "Place this amongst the archives," he said flippantly.

"Why not keep it here?" asked Angel in surprise.

Jimmy walked to one of the three French windows that opened on to a small balcony. He took a rapid survey of the street, then beckoned to Angel. "Do you see that man?" He pointed to a lounger sauntering along on the opposite sidewalk. "Yes."

Jimmy walked back to the centre of the room. "That's why," he said simply. "There will be a burglary here tonight or tomorrow night. People aren't going to let a fortune slip through their fingers without making some kind of effort to save it."

"What people?" demanded the girl. "You mean those dreadful men who took me away?"

"That is very possible," said Jimmy, "although I was thinking of somebody else."

The girl had put on her wrap, and stood irresolutely near the door, and Angel was waiting. "Goodbye," she said hesitatingly. "I—I am afraid I have done you an injustice, and—and I want to thank you for all you have undergone for me. I know—I feel that I have been ungracious, and—"

"You have done me no injustice," said Jimmy in a low voice. "I am all that you thought I was—and worse."

She held out her hand to him, and he raised it to his lips, which was unlike Jimmy.

VIII. — OLD GEORGE

A STRANGER making a call in that portion of North Kensington which lies in the vicinity of Ladbroke Grove by some mischance lost his way. He wandered through many prosperous crescents and quiet squares redolent of the opulence of the upper middle classes, through broad avenues where neat broughams stood waiting in small carriage-drives, and once he blundered into a tidy mews, where horsy men with great hissings made ready the chariots of the Notting Hill plutocracy. It may be that he was in no particular hurry to arrive at his destination, this stranger—who has nothing to do with the story—but certainly he did not avail himself of opportunity in the shape of a passing policeman, and continued his aimless wanderings. He found Kensington Park Road, a broad thoroughfare of huge gardens and walled forecourts, then turned into a side street. He walked about twenty paces, and found himself in the heart of slum-land. It is no ordinary slum this little patch of property that lies between Westbourne Grove and Kensington Park Road. There are no tumbled-down hovels or noisome passages; there are streets of houses dignified with flights of steps that rise to pretentious street doors and areas where long dead menials served the need of the lower middle classes of other days. The streets are given over to an army of squalling children in varying styles of dirtiness, and the halls of these houses are bare of carpet or covering, and in some the responsibility of leasehold is shared by eight or nine families, all pigging together. They are streets of slatternly women, who live at their front doors, arms rolled under discoloured aprons, and on Saturday nights one street at least deserves the pithy but profane appellation which the police have given it—"Little Hell." In this particular thoroughfare it is held that of all sins the greatest is that which is associated—with "spying." A "spy" is a fairly comprehensive phrase in Cawdor Street. It may mean policeman, detective, school—board official, rent collector, or the gentleman appointed by the gas company to extract pennics from the slot-meters.

To Cawdor Street came a man who rented one of the larger houses. To the surprise of the agent, he offered his rent monthly in advance; to the surprise of the street, he took no lodgers. It was the only detached house in that salubrious road, and was No. 49. The furniture came by night, which is customary amongst people who concentrate their last fluttering rag of pride upon the respectability of their household goods. Cawdor Street, on the qui vive for the lady of the house, learns with genuine astonishment that there was none, and that the newcomer was a bachelor. Years ago No. 49 had been the abode of a jobbing builder, hence the little yard gate that flanked one side; and it was with satisfaction that the Cawdor Streeters discovered that the new occupant intended reviving the ancient splendour of the establishment. At any rate, a board was prominently displayed, bearing the inscription:

J. JONES, BUILDER AND CONTRACTOR.

and the inquisitive Mr. Lane (of 76), who caught a momentary vision of the yard through the gate, observed "Office" printed in fairly large letters over the side door. At stated hours, mostly in the evening, roughly-dressed men called at the "Office," stayed a while, and went away. Two dilapidated ladders made their appearance in the yard, conspicuously lifting their perished rungs above the gate level.

"I tried to buy an old builder's cart and wheelbarrow today," said "Mr. Jones" to a workman. "I'll probably get it tomorrow at my own price, and it wouldn't be a bad idea to get a few sacks of lime and a couple of cartloads of sand and bricks in, also a few road pitchers to give it a finishing touch."

The workman grinned. "You've got this place ready in time, Connor," he said. Mr. Connor—for such "J. Jones, Builder and Contractor" was—nodded and picked his teeth meditatively with a match stick.

"I've seen for a long time the other place was useless," he said with a curse. "It was bad luck that Angel found us there last week. I've been fixing up this house for a couple of months. It's a nice neighbourhood, where people don't go nosing around, and the boys can meet here without anybody being the wiser."

"And old George?"

"We'll settle him tonight," said the other with a frown. "Bat is bringing him over, and I want to know how he came to let Angel get at us."

Old George had always been a problem to the "Borough Lot." He held the position of trust that many contended no demented old man should hold.

"Was it safe or sane to trust him with the plate that had been so laboriously acquired from Roebury House, and the jewels of Lady Ivy Task-Hender, for the purloining of which one "Hog" Stander was at that very moment doing seven stretch? Was it wise to install him as custodian of the empty house at Blackwall, through which Angel Esquire gained admittance to the meeting-place of the "Borough Lot"? Some there were who said "Yes," and these included the powerful faction that numbered "Bat" Sands, "Curt" Goyle, and Connor amongst them. They contended that suspicion would never rest on this half-witted old gentleman, with his stuffed birds, his goldfish, caged rabbits and mice, a view that was supported by the fact that Lady Ivy's priceless diamonds lay concealed for months in the false bottom of a hutch devoted to guinea pigs in old George's strange menagerie, what time the police were turning London inside out in their quest for the property."

But now old George was under a cloud. Notwithstanding the fact that he had been found amongst his live stock securely bound to a chair, with a handkerchief over his mouth, suspicion attached to him. How had Angel worked away in the upper room without old George's knowledge? Angel might have easily explained. Indeed, Angel might have relieved their minds to a very large extent in regard to old George, for in marking down the haunt of the "Borough Lot" he had been entirely deceived as to the part played by the old man who acted as "caretaker" to the "empty" house. In a four-wheeled cab old George, smiling foolishly and passing his hand from time to time over his tremulous mouth, listened to the admonitions of Mr. Bat Sands.

"Connor wants to know all about it," said Bat menacingly, "and if you have been playing tricks, old man, the Lord help you."

"The Lord help me," smiled old George complacently. He ran his dirty lingers through his few scanty white locks, and the smile died out of his face, and his loose mouth dropped pathetically.

"Mr. Sands," he said, then stopped; then he repeated the name to himself a dozen times; then he rubbed his head again. Bat, leaning forward to catch what might be a confession, sank back again in his seat and swore softly.

In the house of "J. Jones, Builder and Contractor," were gathered in strength the men who composed the "Borough Lot."

"Suppose he gave us away," asked Goyle, "what shall we do with him?"

There was little doubt as to the feeling of the meeting. A low animal growl, startling in its ferocity, ran through the gathering.

"If he's given us away"—it was Vinnis with his dull fishlike eyes turned upon Connor who was talking—"why, we must 'out' him."

"You're talking like a fool," said Connor contemptuously. "If he has given us away, you may rest assured that he is no sooner in this house than the whole place will be surrounded by police. If Angel knows old George is one of us, he'll be watched day and night, and the cab that brings him will be followed by another bringing Angel. No, I'll stake my life on the old man. But I want to know how Mr. Cursed Angel got into the house next door."

They had not long to wait, for Bat's knock came almost as Connor finished speaking. Half led, half dragged into the room, old George stood, fumbling his hat in his hand, smiling helplessly at the dark faces that met his. He muttered something under his breath. "What's that?" asked Connor sharply. "I said, a gentleman—" began old George, then lapsed into silence. "What gentleman?" asked Connor roughly.

"I am speaking of myself," said the old man, and there came into his face a curious expression of dignity. "I say, and I maintain, that a gentleman is a gentleman whatever company he affects. At my old college I once reproved an undergraduate." He was speaking with stately, almost pompous distinctness. "I said, 'There is an axiom to which I would refer you, De gustibus non est disputandum, and—and—'"

His shaking fingers went up again to the tell-tale mouth, and the vacant smile came back.

"Look here," said Connor, shaking his arm, "we don't want to know anything about your damned college; we want to know how Angel got into our crib."

The old man looked puzzled. "Yes, yes," he muttered; "of course, Mr. Connor, you have been most kind—the crib—ah!—the young man who wanted to rent or hire the room upstairs."

"Yes, yes," said Connor eagerly.

"A most admirable young man," old George rambled on, "but very inquisitive. I remember once, when I was addressing a large congregation of young men at Cheltenham—or it may have been young ladies—"

"Curse the man!" cried Goyle in a fury. "Make him answer, or stop his mouth."

Connor warned him back. "Let him talk in his own way," he said.

"This admirable person," the old man went on, happily striking on the subject again, "desired information that I was not disposed to give, Mr.

Connor, remembering your many kindnesses, particularly in respect to one Mr. Vinnis."

"Yes, go on," urged Connor, and the face of Vinnis was tense.

"I fear there are times when my usually active mind takes on a sluggishness which is foreign to my character—my normal character"—old George was again the pedant—"when the unobservant stranger might be deceived into regarding me as a negligible quantity. The admirable young man so far treated me as such as to remark to his companion that there was a rope—yes, distinctly a rope—for the said Mr. Vinnis."

The face of Vinnis was livid.

"And," asked Connor, "What happened next? There were two of them, were there?"

The old man nodded gravely; he nodded a number of times, as though the exercise pleased him. "The other young man—not the amiable one, but another—upon finding that I could not rent or hire the rooms—as indeed I could not, Mr. Connor, without your permission—engaged me in conversation—very loudly he spoke, too—on the relative values of cabbage and carrot as food for herbaceous mammals. Where the amiable gentleman was at that moment I cannot say—"

"I can guess," thought Connor.

"I can remember the occasion well," old George continued, "because that night I was alarmed and startled by strange noises from the empty rooms upstairs, which I very naturally and properly concluded were caused—" He stopped, and glancing fearfully about the room, went on in a lower tone. "By certain spirits," he whispered mysteriously, and pointed and leered first at one and then another of the occupants of the room. There was something very eerie in the performance of the strange old man with the queerly working face, and more than one hardened criminal present shivered a little.

Connor broke the silence that fell on the room. "So that's how it was done, eh? One held you in conversation while the other got upstairs and hid himself? Well, boys, you've heard the old man. What d'ye say?" Vinnis shifted in his seat and turned his great unemotional face to where the old man stood, still fumbling with his hat and muttering to himself beneath his breath; in some strange region whither his poor wandering mind had taken him he was holding a conversation with an imaginary person. Connor could see his eyebrows working, and caught scraps of sentences, now in some strange dead tongue, now in the stilted English of the schoolmaster. It was Vinnis who spoke for the assembled company.

"The old man knows a darned sight too much," he said in his level tone.

"I'm for—" He did not finish his sentence. Connor took a swift survey of the men. "If there is any man here," he said slowly, "who wants to wake up at seven o'clock in the morning and meet a gentleman who will strap his hands behind him and a person who will pray over him—if there's any man here that wants a short walk after breakfast between two lines of warders to a little shed where a brand new rope is hanging from the roof, he's at liberty to do what he likes with old George, but not in this house."

He fixed his eyes on Vinnis. "And if there's any man here," he went on, "who's already in the shadow of the rope, so that one or two murders more won't make much difference one way or the other, he can do as he likes—outside this house."

Vinnis shrank back. "There's nothing against me," he growled.

"The rope," muttered the old man, "Vinnis for the rope," he chuckled to himself. "I fear they counted too implicitly upon the fact that I am not always quite myself—Vinnis—"

The man he spoke of sprang to his feet with a snarl like a trapped beast.

"Sit down, you." Bat Sands, with his red head close cropped, thrust his chair in the direction of the infuriated Vinnis. "What Connor says is true—we're not going to croak the old man, and we're not going to croak ourselves. If we hang, it will be something worth hanging for. As to the old man, he's soft, an' that's all you can say. He's got to be kept close—"

A rap at the door cut him short. "Who's that?" he whispered.

Connor tiptoed to the locked door. "Who's there?" he demanded.

A familiar voice reassured him, and he opened the door and held a conversation in a low voice with somebody outside. "There's a man who wants to see me," he said in explanation. "Lock the door after I leave, Bat," and he went out quickly. Not a word was spoken, but each after his own fashion of reasoning drew some conclusion from Connor's hasty departure.

"A full meetin'," croaked a voice from the back of the room. "We're all asked here by Connor. Is it a plant?"

That was Bat's thought too. "No," he said; "there's nothin' against us. Why, Angel let us off only last week because there wasn't evidence, an' Connor's straight."

"I don't trust him, by God!" said Vinnis. "I trust nobody," said Bat doggedly, "but Connor's straight—"

There was a rap on the door. "Who's there?"

"All right!" said the muffled voice. Bat unlocked the door, and Connor came in. What he had seen or what he had heard had brought about a marvellous change in his appearance—his cheeks were a dull red, and his eyes blazed with triumph. "Boys," he said, and they caught the infectious thrill in his voice, "I've got the biggest thing for you—a million pounds, share and share alike."

He felt rather than heard the excitement his words caused. He stood with his back to the half-opened door.

"I'm going to introduce a new pal," he rattled on breathlessly. "I'll vouch for him."

"Who is he?" asked Bat. "Do we know him?"

"No," said Connor, "and you're not expected to know him. But he's putting up the money, and that's good enough for you, Bat—a hundred pounds a man, and it will be paid tonight." Bat Sands spat on his hand. "Bring him in. He's good enough," and there was a murmur of approval. Connor disappeared for a moment, and returned followed by a well-dressed stranger, who met the questioning glances of his audience with a quiet smile.

His eyes swept over every face. They rested for a moment on Vinnis, they looked doubtfully at old George, who, seated on a chair with crossed legs and his head bent, was talking with great rapidity in an undertone to himself.

"Gentlemen," said the stranger, "I have come with the object of gaining your help. Mr. Connor has told me that he has already informed you about Reale's millions. Briefly, I have decided to forestall other people, and secure the money for myself. I offer you a half share of the money, to be equally divided amongst you, and as an earnest of my intention, I am paying each man who is willing to help me a hundred pounds down."

He drew from one of his pockets a thick package of notes, and from two other pockets similar bundles. He handed them to Connor, and the hungry eyes of the "Borough Lot" focused upon the crinkling paper.

"What I shall ask you to do," the stranger proceeded, "I shall tell you later—"

"Wait a bit," interrupted Bat. "Who else is in this?"

"We alone," replied the man.

"Is Jimmy in it?"

"No."

"Is Angel in it?"

"No" (impatiently).

"Go on," said Bat, satisfied.

"The money is in a safe that can only be opened by a word. That word nobody knows—so far. The clue to the word was stolen a few nights ago from the lawyer in charge of the case by—Jimmy." He paused to note the effect of his words.

"Jimmy has passed the clue on to Scotland Yard, and we cannot hope to get it."

"Well?" demanded Bat.

"What we can do," the other went on, "is to open the safe with something more powerful than a word."

"But the guard!" said Bat. "There's an armed guard kept there by the lawyer."

"We can arrange about the guard," said the other.

"Why not get at the lawyer?" It was Curt Goyle who made the suggestion.

The stranger frowned. "The lawyer cannot be got at," he said shortly. "Now, are you with me?"

There was no need to ask. Connor was sorting the notes into little bundles on the table, and the men came up one by one, took their money, and after a few words with Connor took their leave, with an awkward salutation to the stranger.

Bat was the last to go. "Tomorrow night—here," muttered Connor.

He was left alone with the newcomer, save for the old man, who hadn't changed his attitude, and was still in the midst of some imaginary conversation.

"Who is this?" the stranger demanded.

Connor smiled. "An old chap as mad as a March hare. A gentleman, too, and a scholar; talks all sorts of mad languages—Latin and Greek and the Lord knows what. He's been a schoolmaster, I should say, and what brought him down to this—drink or drugs or just ordinary madness—I don't know."

The stranger looked with interest at the unconscious man, and old George, as if suddenly realizing that he was under scrutiny, woke up with a start and sat blinking at the other. Then he shuffled slowly to his feet and peered closely into the stranger's face, all the time sustaining his mumbled conversation.

"Ah," he said in a voice rising from its inaudibility, "a gentleman! Pleased to meet you, sir, pleased to meet you. Omnia mutantur, nos et mutamur in illis, but you have not changed." He relapsed again into mutterings.

"I have never met him before," the stranger said, turning to Connor.

"Oh, old George always thinks he has met people," said Connor with a grin.

"A gentleman," old George muttered, "every inch a gentleman, and a munificent patron. He bought a copy of my book—you have read it? It is called—dear me, I have forgotten what it is called—and sent to consult me in his—ah !—anagram—"

"What?" The stranger's face was ashen, and he gripped Connor by the arm.

"Listen, listen!" he whispered fiercely. Old George threw up his head again and stared blandly at the stranger.

"A perfect gentleman," he said with pathetic insolence, "invariably addressing me as the 'professor'—a most delicate and gentlemanly thing to do."

He pointed a triumphant linger to the stranger. "I know you!" he cried shrilly, and his cracked laugh rang through the room. "Spedding, that's your name! Lawyer, too. I saw you in the carriage of my patron."

"The book, the book!" gasped Spedding. "What was the name of your book?" Old George's voice had dropped to its normal level when he replied with extravagant courtesy—"That is the one thing, sir, I can never remember."

IX. — THE GREAT ATTEMPT

THERE are supercilious critics who sneer at Scotland Yard. They are quite unofficial critics, of course, writers of stories wherein figure amateur detectives of abnormal perspicuity, unravelling mysteries with consummate ease which have baffled the police for years. As a matter of fact, Scotland Yard stands for the finest police organization in the world. People who speak glibly of "police blunders" might remember one curious fact: in this last quarter of a century only one man has ever stood in the dock at the Old Bailey under the capital charge who has escaped the dread sentence of the law. Scotland Yard is patiently slow and terribly sure.

Angel in his little room received a letter written in a sprawling, uneducated hand; it was incoherent and stained with tears and underlined from end to end. He read it through and examined the date stamp, then rang his bell. The messenger who answered him found him examining a map of London.

"Go to the Record Office, and get EB. 93", he said, and in five minutes the messenger came back with a thick folder bulging with papers. There were newspaper cuttings and plans and dreadful photographs, the like of which the outside world do not see, and there was a little key ticketed with an inscription.

Angel looked through the dossier carefully, then read the woman's letter again ...

Vinnis, the man with the dead-white face, finishing his late breakfast, and with the pleasurable rustle of new banknotes in his trouser pocket, strolled forth into Commercial Road, E. An acquaintance leaning against a public-house gave him a curt nod of recognition; a bedraggled girl hurrying homeward with her man's breakfast in her apron shrank on one side, knowing Vinnis to her sorrow; a stray cur cringed up to him, as he stood for a moment at the edge of the road, and was kicked for its pains. Vinnis was entirely without sentiment, and besides, even though the money in his pocket compensated for most things, the memory of old George and his babbling talk worried him.

Somebody on the other side of the road attracted his attention. It was a woman, and he knew her very well, therefore he ignored her beckoning hand. Two days ago he had occasion to reprove her, and he had seized the opportunity to summarily dissolve the informal union that had kept them together for five years. So he made no sign when the woman with the bruised face called him, but turned abruptly and walked towards Aldgate. He did not look round, but by and by he heard the patter of her feet behind, and once his name called hoarsely. He struck off into a side street with a raging devil inside him, then when they reached an unfrequented part of the road he turned on her.

She saw the demon in his eyes, and tried to speak. She was a penitent woman at that moment, and hysterically ripe for confession, but the savage menace of the man froze her lips.

"So," he said, his thin mouth askew, "so after what I've said an' what I've done you follow me, do you. Showing me up in the street, eh!" He edged closer to her, his fist doubled, and she, poor drab, fascinated by the snakelike glare of his dull eyes, stood rooted to the spot. Then with a snarl he struck her—once, twice—and she fell a huddled, moaning heap on the pavement.

You may do things in Commercial Road, E., after "lighting-up time" that are not permissible in the broad light of the day, unless it be Saturday, and the few people who had been attracted by the promise of a row were indignant but passive, after the manner of all London crowds. Not so one quiet, middle-aged man, who confronted Vinnis as he began to walk away.

"That was a particularly brutal thing to do," said the quiet man. Vinnis measured him with his eye, and decided that this was not a man to be trifled with.

"I've got nothing to say to you," he said roughly, and tried to push past, but an iron grip was on his arm.

"Wait a moment, my friend," said the other steadily, "not so fast; you cannot commit a brutal assault in the open street like that without punishment. I must ask you to walk with me to the station."

"Suppose I won't go?" demanded Vinnis.

"I shall take you," said the other. "I am Detective-Sergeant Jarvis from Scotland Yard."

Vinnis thought rapidly. There wasn't much chance of escape; the street they were in was a cul-de-sac, and at the open end two policemen had made their appearance. After all, a "wife" assault was not a serious business, and the woman—well, she would swear it was an accident. He resolved to go quietly; at the worst it would be a month, so with a shrug of his shoulders he accompanied the detective. A small crowd followed them to the station. In the little steel dock he stood in his stockinged feet whilst a deft jailer ran his hands over him. With a stifled oath, he remembered the money in his possession; it was only ten pounds, for he had secreted the other, but ten pounds is a lot of money to be found on a person of his class, and generally leads to embarrassing inquiries. To his astonishment, the jailer who relieved him of the notes seemed in no whit surprised, and the inspector at the desk took the discovery as a matter of course. Vinnis remarked on the surprising number of constables there were on duty in the charge room. Then—"What is the charge?" asked the inspector, dipping his pen. "Wilful murder!" said a voice, and Angel Esquire crossed the room from the inspector's office. "I charge this man with having on the night of the 17th of February... " Vinnis, dumb with terror and rage, listened to the crisp tones of the detective as he detailed the particulars of an almost forgotten crime. It was the story of a country house burglary, a man-servant who surprised the thief, a light in the dark, a shot and a dead man lying in the big drawing-room. It was an ordinary little tragedy, forgotten by everybody save Scotland Yard; but year by year unknown men had pieced together the scraps of evidence that had come to them; strand by strand had the rope been woven that was to hang a cold-blooded murderer; last of all came the incoherent letter from a jealous woman—Scotland Yard waits always for a jealous woman—and the evidence was complete.

"Put him in No. 14", said the inspector. Then Vinnis woke up, and the six men on duty in the charge room found their time fully occupied. Vinnis was arrested, as Angel Esquire put it, "in the ordinary way of business."

Hundreds of little things happen daily at Scotland Yard in the ordinary way of business which, apparently unconnected one with the other, have an extraordinary knack of being in some remote fashion related. A burglary at Clapham was remarkable for the fact that a cumbersome mechanical toy was carried away in addition to other booty. A street accident in the Kingsland Road led to the arrest of a drunken carman. In the excitement of the moment a sneak-thief purloined a parcel from the van, was chased and captured. A weeping wife at the police station gave him a good character as husband and father. "Only last week he brought my boy a fine performin' donkey," An alert detective went home with her, recognized the mechanical toy from the description, and laid by the heels the notorious "Kingsland Road Lot."

The arrest of Vinnis was totally unconnected with Angel's investigations into the mystery of Reale's millions. He knew him as a "Borough man," but did not associate him with the search for the word. None the less, there are certain formalities attached to the arrest of all bad criminals. Angel Esquire placed one or two minor matters in the hands of subordinates, and in two days one of these waited upon him in his office. "The notes, sir," said the man, "were issued to Mr. Spedding on his private account last Monday morning. Mr. Spedding is a lawyer, of the firm of Spedding, Mortimer and Larach."

"Have you seen Mr. Spedding?" he asked. "Yes, sir. Mr. Spedding remembers drawing the money and paying it away to a gentleman who was sailing to America."

"A client?"

"So far as I can gather," said the subordinate, "the money was paid on behalf of a client for services. Mr. Spedding would not particularize."

Angel Esquire made a little grimace. "Lawyers certainly do queer things," he said dryly. "Does Mr. Spedding offer any suggestion as to how the money came into this man's possession?"

"No, sir. He thinks he might have obtained it quite honestly. I understand that the man who received the money was a shady sort of customer."

"So I should imagine," said Angel Esquire. Left alone, he sat in deep thought drawing faces on his blotting—pad. Then he touched a bell.

"Send Mr. Carter to me," he directed, and in a few minutes a bright-faced youth, lingering an elementary moustache, was awaiting his orders.

"Carter," said Angel cautiously, "it must be very dull work in the finger-print department?"

"I don't know, sir," said the other, a fairly enthusiastic ethnologist, "we've got-"

"Carter," said Angel more cautiously still, "are you on for a lark?"

"Like a bird, sir," said Carter, unconsciously humorous.

"I want a dozen men, the sort of men who won't talk to reporters, and will remain 'unofficial' so long as I want them to be," said Angel, and he unfolded his plan. When the younger man had gone Angel drew a triangle on the blotting-pad. "Spedding is in with the 'Borough Lot'", he put a cross against one angle.

"Spedding knows I know," he put a cross at the apex. "I know that Spedding knows I know," he marked the remaining angle. "It's Spedding's move, and he'll move damn quick."

The Assistant Commissioner came into the room at that moment.

"Hullo, Angel!" he said, glancing at the figures on the pad. "What's this, a new game?"

"It's an old game," said Angel truthfully, "but played in an entirely new way."

Angel was not far wrong when he surmised that Spedding's move would be immediate, and although the detective had reckoned without an unknown factor, in the person of old George, yet a variety of circumstances combined to precipitate the act that Angel anticipated. Not least of these was the arrest of Vinnis. After his interview with old George, Spedding had decided on a waiting policy. The old man had been taken to the house at Clapham. Spedding had been prepared to wait patiently until some freak of mind brought back the memory to the form of cryptogram he had advised. A dozen times a day he asked the old man—"What is your name?"

"Old George, only old George," was the invariable reply, with many grins and noddings."

"But your real name, the name you had when you were a professor." But this would only start the old man off on a rambling reminiscence of his "munificent patron."

Connor came secretly to Clapham for orders. It was the night after Vinnis had been arrested. "We've got to move at once, Mr. Connor," said the lawyer. Connor sat in the chair that had held Jimmy a few nights previous.

"It is no use waiting for the old man to talk, the earlier plan was best."

"Has anything happened?" asked Connor. His one-time awe of the lawyer had merged in the familiarity of conspiratorship.

"There was a detective at my office today inquiring about some notes that were found on Vinnis. Angel Esquire will draw his own conclusions, and we have no time to lose."

"We are ready," said Connor. "Then let it be tomorrow night. I will withdraw the guard of commissionaires at the safe. I can easily justify myself afterwards."

An idea struck Connor. "Why not send another lot of men to relieve them? I can fix up some of the boys so that they'll look like commissionaires."

Spedding's eyes narrowed. "Yes," he said slowly, "it could be arranged—an excellent idea." He paced the room with long, swinging strides, his forehead puckered. "There are two reliefs," he said, "one in the morning and one in the evening. I could send a note to the sergeant of the morning relief telling him that I had arranged for a new set of night men—I have changed them twice already, one cannot be too careful—and I could give you the necessary authority to take over charge."

"Better still," said Connor, "instruct him to withdraw, leaving the place empty, then our arrival will attract no notice. Lombard Street must be used to the commissionaires going on guard."

"That is an idea," said Spedding, and sat down to write the letter.

The night of the great project turned out miserably wet. "So much the better," muttered Connor, viewing the world from his Kensington fastness. The room dedicated to the use of the master of the house was plainly furnished, and on the bare deal table Connor had set his whisky down whilst he peered through the rain-blurred windows at the streaming streets.

"England for work and Egypt for pleasure," he muttered; "and if I get my share of the money, and it will be a bigger share than my friend Spedding imagines, it's little this cursed country will see of Mr. Patrick Connor."

He drained oft his whisky at a gulp, rubbed the steam from the windows, and looked down into the deserted street. Two men were walking toward the house. One, well covered by a heavy mackintosh cloak, moved with a long stride; the other, wrapped in a new overcoat, shuffled by his side, quickening his steps to keep up with his more energetic companion.

"Spedding," said Connor, "and old George. What is he bringing him here for?" He hurried downstairs to let them in. "Well?" asked Spedding, throwing his reeking coat off.

"All's ready," answered Connor. "Why have you brought the old man?"

"Oh, for company," the lawyer answered carelessly. If the truth be told, Spedding still hoped that the old man would remember. That day old George had been exceedingly garrulous, almost lucidly so at times. Mr. Spedding still held on to the faint hope that the old man's revelations would obviate the necessity for employing the "Borough Lot," and what was more important, for sharing the contents of the safe with them. As to this latter part of the program, Mr. Spedding had plans which would have astonished Connor had he but known. But old George's loquacity stopped short at the all-important point of instructing the lawyer on the question of the cryptogram. He had brought him along in the hope that at the eleventh hour the old man would reveal his identity. Unconscious of the responsibility that lay upon his foolish head, the old man sat in the upstairs room communing with himself.

"We will leave him here," said the lawyer, "he will be safe."

"Safe enough. I know him of old. He'll sit here for hours amusing himself."

"And now, what about the men?" asked the lawyer. "Where do we meet them?"

"We shall pick them up at the corner of Lombard Street, and they'll follow me to the Safe Deposit."

"Ah!" They turned swiftly on old George, who with his chin raised and with face alert was staring at them. "Safe Deposit, Lombard Street," he mumbled. "And a most excellent plan too—a most excellent plan."

The two men held their breath. "And quite an ingenious idea, sir. Did you say Lombard Street—a safe?" he muttered. "A safe with a word? And how to conceal the word, that's the question. I am a man of honour, you may trust me." He made a sweeping bow to some invisible presence. "Why not conceal your word thus?" Old George stabbed the palm of his hand with a grimy forefinger.

"Why not? Have you read my book? It is only a little book, but useful, sir, remarkably useful. The drawings and the signs are most accurate. An eminent gentleman at the British Museum assisted me in its preparation. It is called—it is called—" He passed his hand wearily over his head, and slid down into his chair again, a miserable old man muttering foolishly.

Spedding wiped the perspiration from his forehead. "Nearly, nearly!" he said huskily. "By Heavens! he nearly told us."

Connor looked at him with suspicion.

"What's all this about the book?" he demanded. "This is the second time old George has spoken like this. It's to do with old Reale, isn't it?"

Spedding nodded.

"Come," said Connor, looking at his watch, "it's time we were moving. We'll leave the old man to look after the house. Here, George."

Old George looked up. "You'll stay here, and not leave till we return. D'ye hear?"

"I hear, Mr. Connor, sir," said old George, with his curious assumption of dignity, "and hearing, obey."

As the two men turned into the night the rain pelted down and a gusty northwesterly wind blew into their faces.

"George," said Connor, answering a question, "oh, we've had him for years. One of the boys found him wandering about Limehouse with hardly any clothes to his back, and brought him to us. That was before I knew the 'Borough Lot,' but they used him as a blind. He was worth the money it cost to keep him in food."

Spedding kept the other waiting whilst he dispatched a long telegram from the Westbourne Grove Post Office. It was addressed to the master of the Polecat lying at Cardiff, and was reasonably unintelligible to the clerk. They found a hansom at the corner of Queen's Road, and drove to the Bank; here they alighted and crossed to the Royal Exchange. Some men in uniform overcoats who were standing about exchanged glances with Connor, and as the two leaders doubled back to Lombard Street, followed them at a distance.

"The guard left at four o'clock," said Spedding, fitting the key of the heavy outer door. He waited a few minutes in the inky black darkness of the vestibule whilst Connor admitted the six uniformed men who had followed them.

"Are we all here?" said Connor in a low voice. "Bat? Here! Goyle? Here! Lamby? Here!" One by one he called them by their names and they answered.

"We may as well have a light," said Spedding, and felt for the switch. The gleam of the electric lamps showed Spedding as pure a collection of scoundrels as ever disgraced the uniform of a gallant corps.

"Now," said Spedding in level tones, "are all the necessary tools here?"

Bat's grin was the answer. "If we can get an electric connection," he said, "we'll burn out the lock of the safe in half—"

Spedding had walked to the inner door that led to the great hall, and was fumbling with the keys. Suddenly he started back. "Hark!" he whispered. "I heard a step in the hall."

Connor listened. "I hear nothing," he began, when the inner door was thrown open, and a commissionaire, revolver in hand, stepped out.

"Stand!" he cried. Then, recognizing Spedding, dropped the muzzle of his pistol.

White with rage, Spedding stood amidst his ill-assorted bodyguard. In the searching white light of the electric lamps there was no mistaking their character. He saw the commissionaire eying them curiously.

"I understood," he said slowly, "that the guard had been relieved."

"No, sir," said the man, and the cluster of uniformed men at the door of the inner hall confirmed this.

"I sent orders this afternoon," said Spedding between his teeth.

"No orders have been received, sir," and the lawyer saw the scrutinizing eye of the soldierly sentry pass over his confederates. "Is this the relief?" asked the guard, not attempting to conceal the contempt in his tone.

"Yes," said the lawyer.

As the sentry saluted and disappeared into the hall Spedding drew Connor aside.

"This is ruin," he said quickly. "The safe must be cleared tonight. Tomorrow London will not hold me."

The sentry reappeared at the doorway and beckoned them in. They shuffled into the great hall, where in the half darkness the safe loomed up from its rocky pedestal, an eerie, mysterious thing. He saw Bat Sands glancing uncomfortably around the dim spaces of the building, and felt the impression of the loneliness.

A man who wore the stripes of a sergeant came up.

"Are we to withdraw, sir?" he asked.

"Yes," said Spedding shortly.

"Will you give us a written order?" asked the man.

Spedding hesitated, then drew out a pocket-book and wrote a few hasty words on a sheet, tore it out, and handed it to the man. The sergeant looked at it carefully.

"You haven't signed it or dated it either," he said respectfully, and handed it back. Spedding cursed him under his breath and rectified the omissions.

"Now you may go." In the half-light, for only one solitary electrolier illuminated the vast hall, he thought the man was smiling. It might have been a trick of the shadows, for he could not see his face.

"And am I to leave you alone?" said the sergeant.

"Yes."

"Is it safe?" the non-commissioned officer asked quietly.

"Curse you, what do you mean?" cried the lawyer.

"Well," said the other easily, "I see you have Connor with you, a notorious thief and blackmailer." The lawyer was dumb. "And Bat Sands. How d'ye do, Bat? How did they treat you in Borstal, or was it Parkhurst?" drawled the sergeant.

"And there's the gentle Lamby trying hard to look military in an overcoat too large for him. That's not the uniform you're used to wearing, Lamby, eh?" From the group of men at the door came a genuinely amused laugh.

"Guard the outer door, one of you chaps," said the sergeant, and turning again to Spedding's men, "Here we have our respected friend Curt Goyle." He stooped and picked up a bag that Bat had placed gingerly on the floor. "What a bag of tricks," the sergeant cooed, "diamond bits and dynamite cartridges and—what's this little thing, Bat—an ark? It is. By Jove, I congratulate you on the swag."

Spedding had recovered his nerve and strode forward. He was playing for the greatest stake in the world. "You shall be punished for this insolence," he stormed.

"Not at all," said the imperturbable sergeant.

Somebody at the door spoke. "Here's another one, sergeant," and pushed a queer old figure into the hall, a figure that blinked and peered from face to face.

He espied Spedding, and ran up to him almost fawning.

"The Safe Deposit—in Lombard Street," he cackled joyously. "You see, I remembered, dear friend; and I've come to tell you about the book—my book, you know. My munificent patron who desired a puzzle word—"

The sergeant started forward. "My God!" he cried, "the professor."

"Yes, yes," chuckled the old man, "that's what he called me. He bought a copy of my book—two sovereigns, four sovereigns he gave me. The book— what was it called?" The old man paused and clasped both hands to his head.

"A Study—a Study," he said painfully, "on the Origin of—the Alphabet. Ah!"

Another of the commissionaires had come forward as the old man began speaking, and to him the sergeant turned.

"Make a note of that, Jimmy," the sergeant said.

Spedding reeled back as though he had been struck.

"Angel!" he gasped.

"That's me," was the ungrammatical reply.

Crushed, cowed, beaten and powerless, Spedding awaited judgment.

What form it would take he could not guess, that it would effectively ruin him he did not doubt. The trusted lawyer stood self-condemned; there was no explaining away his companions, there could be no mistaking the meaning of their presence.

"Send your men away," said Angel. A wild hope seized the lawyer. The men were not to be arrested, there was a chance for him. The "Borough Lot" needed no second ordering; they trooped through the doorway, anxious to reach the open air before Angel changed his mind.

"You may go," said Angel to Connor, who still lingered.

"If the safe is to be opened, I'm in it," was the sullen reply.

"You may go," said Angel; "the safe will not be opened tonight."

"I—"

"Go!" thundered the detective, and Connor slunk away.

Angel beckoned the commissionaire who had first interrogated Spedding.

"Take charge of that bag, Carter. There are all sorts of things in it that go off." Then he turned to the lawyer. "Mr. Spedding, there is a great deal that I have to say to you, but it would be better to defer our conversation; the genuine guard will return in a few minutes. I told them to return at 10 o'clock."

"By what authority?" blustered Spedding.

"Tush!" said Angel wearily. "Surely we have got altogether beyond that stage. Your order for withdrawal was expected by me. I waited upon the sergeant of the guard with another order."

"A forged order, I gather?" said Spedding, recovering his balance. "Now I see why you have allowed my men to go. I overrated your generosity."

"The order," said Angel soberly, "was signed by His Majesty's Secretary of State for Home Affairs"—he tapped the astonished lawyer on the shoulder—"and if it would interest you to know, I have a warrant in my pocket for the arrest of every man jack of you. That I do not put it into execution is a matter of policy."

The lawyer scanned the calm face of the detective in bewilderment.

"What do you want of me?" he asked at length.

"Your presence at Jimmy's flat at ten o'clock tomorrow morning," replied Angel.

"I will be there," said the other, and turned to go.

"And, Mr. Spedding," called Jimmy, as the lawyer reached the door, "in regard to a boat you have chartered from Cardiff, I think you need not go any further in the matter. One of my men is at present interviewing the captain, and pointing out to him the enormity of the offence of carrying fugitives from justice to Spanish-American ports."

"Damn you!" said Spedding, and slammed the door.

Jimmy removed the commissionaire's cap from his head and grinned. "One of these fine days, Angel, you'll lose your job, introducing the Home Secretary's name. Phew!"

"It had to be done," said Angel sadly. "It hurts me to lie, but I couldn't very well tell Spedding that the sergeant of the commissionaires had been one of my own men all along, could I?"

X. — SOME BAD CHARACTERS

IT happened that on the night of the great attempt the inquisitive Mr. Lane, of 76 Cawdor Street, was considerably exercised in his mind as to the depleted condition of his humble treasury. With Mr. Lane the difference between affluence and poverty was a matter of shillings. His line of business was a humble one. Lead piping and lengths of telephone wire, an occasional door-mat improvidently left outside whilst the servant cleaned the hall, these represented the scope and extent of his prey. Perhaps he reached his zenith when he lifted an overcoat from a hatstand what time a benevolent old lady was cutting him thick slices of bread and butter in a basement kitchen. Mr. Lane had only recently returned from a short stay in Wormwood Scrubbs Prison. It was over a trifling affair of horsehair abstracted from railway carriage cushions that compelled Mr. Lane's retirement for two months. It was that same affair that brought about his undoing on the night of the attempt. For the kudos of the railway theft had nerved him to more ambitious attempts, and with a depleted exchequer to urge him forward, and the prestige of his recent achievements to support him, he decided upon burglary. It was a wild and reckless departure from his regular line, and he did not stop to consider the disabilities attaching to a change of profession, nor debate the unpropitious conditions of an already overstocked labour market. It is reasonable to suppose that Mr. Lane lacked the necessary qualities of logic and balance to argue any point to its obvious conclusion, for he was, intellectually, the reverse of brilliant, and was therefore ill-equipped for introspective or psychological examination of the circumstances leading to his decision. Communing with himself, the inquisitive Mr. Lane put the matter tersely and brutally.

"Lead pipin's no go unless you've got a pal to r work with; telephone wires is so covered up with wood casin' that it's worse'n hard work to pinch two-penn'oth. I'm goin' to have a cut at Joneses."

So in the pelting rain he watched "Joneses" from a convenient doorway. He noted with satisfaction the "workmen" departing one by one; he observed with joy the going of "Jones" himself; and when, some few minutes afterwards, the queer-looking old man, whom he suspected as being a sort of caretaker, came shuffling out, slamming the gate behind him, and peering left and right, and mumbling to himself as he squelched through the rain, the watcher regarded the removal of this final difficulty as being an especial act of Providence. He waited for another half hour, because, for some reason or other, the usually deserted street became annoyingly crowded. First came a belated coal cart and a miserably bedraggled car-man who cried his wares dolefully. Then a small boy, escaping from the confines of his domestic circle, came to revel in the downpour and wade ecstatically but thoroughly through the puddles that had formed on the uneven surface of the road. Nemesis, in the shape of a shrill-voiced mother, overtook the boy and sent him whining and expectant to the heavy hand of maternal authority.

With the coast clear Mr. Lane lost no time. In effecting an entrance to the head-quarters of the "Borough Lot," Mr. Lane's method lacked subtlety. He climbed over the gate leading to the yard, trusting inwardly that he was not observed, but taking his chance. Had he been an accomplished burglar, with the experience of any exploits behind him, he would have begun by making a very thorough inspection of likely windows. Certainly he would never have tried the "office" door. Being the veriest tyro, and being conscious, moreover, that his greatest feats had connection with doors carelessly left ajar, he tried the door, and to his delight it opened. Again the skilled craftsman would have suspected some sort of treachery, and might have withdrawn; but Mr. Lane, recognizing in the fact that the old man had forgotten to fasten the door behind him only yet another proof of that benevolent Providence which exerts itself for the express service of men "in luck," entered boldly. He lit a candle stump and looked around. The evidence of that wealth which is the particular possession of "master-men" was not evident. Indeed, the floor of the passage was uncarpeted, and the walls bare of picture or ornament. Nor was the "office," a little room leading from the "passage," any more prolific of result. Such fixtures as there were had apparently been left behind by the previous tenant, and these were thick with dust. "Bah!" said the inquisitive Mr. Lane scornfully, and his words echoed hollowly as in an empty house. With the barren possibilities of his exploit before him, Mr. Lane's spirits fell. He was of the class, to whom reference has already been made, that looked in awe and reverence toward the "Borough Lot" in the same spirit as the youthful curate might regard the consistory of bishops. In his cups—pewter cups they were with frothing heads a- top—he was wont to boast that his connection with the "Borough Lot" was both close and intimate. A rumour that went around to the effect that the "mouthpiece" who defended him at the closing of the unsatisfactory horsehair episode had been paid for by the "Borough Lot" he did not trouble to contradict. If he had known any of them, even by sight, he would not at that moment have been effecting p a burglarious entry into their premises. Room after room he searched. He found the ill-furnished bedroom of Connor, and the room where old George slept on an uncleanly mattress. He found, too, the big room where the "Lot" held their informal meetings, but nothing portable. Nothing that a man might slip under his coat, and walk boldly out of the front door with.

He heard another voice speaking in a lower tone.

"What are we worth? You're a fool! What d'ye think we're worth? Ain't we the 'Borough Lot'? Don't he know enough to hang two or three of us... It's Connor and his pal the lawyer... "

'The Borough Lot'! The paralyzing intelligence came to Mr. Lane, and he held on to the bare mantelshelf for support. Spies! Suppose they discovered him, and mistook him for a spy! His hair rose at the thought. He knew them well enough by repute. Overmuch hero-worship had invested them with qualities for evil which they may or may not have possessed. There might be a chance of escape. The tumult below continued. Scraps of angry talk came floating up. Mr. Lane looked out of the window; the drop into the street was too long, and there was no sign of rope in the house. Cautiously he opened the door of the room. The men were in the room beneath that in which he stood. The staircase that led to the street must take him past their door. Mr. Lane was very anxious to leave the house. He had unwittingly stepped into a hornets' nest, and wanted to make his escape without disturbing the inmates. Now was the time—or never. Whilst the angry argument continued a creaking stair board or so might not attract attention. But he made no allowance for the gifts of these men—gifts of sight and hearing. Bat Sands, in the midst of his tirade, saw the uplifted finger and head-jerk of Goyle. He did not check his flow of invective, but edged toward the door; then he stopped short, and flinging the door open, he caught the scared Mr. Lane by the throat, and dragging him into the rom, threw him upon the ground and knelt on him.

"What are ye doing here?" he whispered fiercely.

Mr. Lane, with protruding eyes, saw the pitiless faces about him, saw Goyle lift a life-preserver from the table and turn half-round the better to strike, and fainted.

"Stop that!" growled Bat, with outstretched hand. "The little swine has fainted. Who is he? Do any of you fellers know him?"

It was the wizened-faced man whom Angel had addressed as Lamby who furnished the identification. "He's a little crook—name of Lane."

"Where does he come from?"

"Oh, hereabouts. He was in the Scrubbs in my time," said Lamby. They regarded the unconscious burglar in perplexity.

"Go through his pockets," suggested Goyle. It happened—and this was the most providential happening of the day from Mr. Lane's point of view—that when he had decided upon embarking on his career of high-class crime he had thoughtfully provided himself with a few home-made instruments. It was the little poker with flattened end to form a jemmy and the centre-bit that was found in his pocket that in all probability saved Mr. Lane's life. Lombroso and other great criminologists have given it out that your true degenerate has no sense of humour, but on two faces at least there was a broad grin when the object of the little man's visit was revealed.

"He came to burgle Connor," said Bat admiringly. "Here, pass over the whisky, one of ye!" He forced a little down the man's throat, and Mr. Lane blinked and opened his eyes in a frightened stare.

"Stand up," commanded Bat, "an' give an account of yourself, young feller. What d'ye mean by breaking into—"

"Never mind about that," Goyle interrupted savagely. "What has he heard when he was sneaking outside—that's the question."

"Nothin', gentlemen!" gasped the unfortunate Mr. Lane, "on me word, gentlemen! I've been in trouble like yourselves, an'—" He realized he had blundered.

"Oh," said Goyle with ominous calm, "so you've been in trouble like us, have you?"

"I mean—"

"I know what you mean," hissed the other; "you mean you've been listenin' to what we've been saying, you little skunk, and you're ready to bleat to the first copper." It might have gone hard with Mr. Lane but for the opportune arrival of the messenger. Bat went downstairs at the knock, and the rest stood quietly listening. They expected Connor, and when his voice did not sound on the stairs they looked at one another questioningly. Bat came into the room with a yellow envelope in his hand. He passed it to Goyle. Reading was not an accomplishment of his. Goyle read it with difficulty.

"Do the best you can," he read. "I'm lying' doggo.'"

"What does that mean?" snarled Goyle, holding the message in his hand and looking at Bat.

"Hidin', is he—and we've got to do the best we can?"

Bat reached for his overcoat. He did not speak as he struggled into it, nor until he had buttoned it deliberately.

"It means—git," he said shortly. "It means run, or else it means time, an' worse than time."

He swung round to the door. "Connor's hidin'," he stopped to say. "When Connor starts hiding the place is getting hot. There's nothing against me so far as I know, except—"

His eyes fell on the form of Mr. Lane. He had raised himself to a sitting position on the floor, and now, with dishevelled hair and outstretched legs, he sat the picture of despair.

Goyle intercepted the glance. "What about him?" he asked.

"Leave him," said Bat; "we've got no time for fooling with him."

A motor-car came buzzing down Cawdor Street, which was unusual. They heard the grind of its brakes outside the door, and that in itself was sufficiently alarming. Bat extinguished the light, and cautiously opened the shutters. He drew back with an oath.

"What's that?" Goyle whispered. Bat made no reply, and they heard him open his matchbox.

"What are you doing?" whispered Goyle fiercely.

"Light the lamp," said the other. The tinkle of glass followed as he removed the chimney, and in the yellow light Bat faced the "Borough Lot." "U—P spells 'up,' an' that's what the game is," he said calmly.

He was searching his pockets as he spoke. "I want a light because there's one or two things in my pocket that I've got to burn—quick!"

After some fumbling he found a paper. He gave it a swift examination, then he struck a match and carefully lit the corner.

"It's the fairest cop," he went on. "The street's full of police, and Angel ain't playing 'gamblin' raids' this time."

There was a heavy knock on the door, but nobody moved.

Goyle's face had gone livid. He knew better than any man there how impossible escape was. That had been one of the drawbacks to the house—the ease with which it could be surrounded. He had pointed out the fact to Connor before.

Again the knock. "Let 'em open it," said Bat grimly, and as though the people outside had heard the invitation, the door crashed in, and there came a patter as of men running on the stairs.

First to enter the room was Angel. He nodded to Bat coolly, then stepped aside to allow the policemen to follow.

"I want you," he said briefly.

"What for?" asked Sands.

"Breaking and entering," said the detective. "Put out your hands!"

Bat obeyed. As the steel stirrup-shaped irons snapped on his wrists he asked—

"Have you got Connor?"

Angel smiled. "Connor lives to fight another day," he said quietly. The policemen who attended him were busy with the other occupants of the room.

"Bit of a field-day for you, Mr. Angel," said the thin-faced Lamby pleasantly.

"Thought you was goin' to let us off?"

"Jumping at conclusions hastily is a habit to be deplored," said Angel sententiously. Then he saw the panic-stricken Mr. Lane.

"Hullo, what's this?" he demanded. Mr. Lane had at that moment the inspiration of his life. Since he was by fortuitous circumstances involved in this matter, and since it could make very little difference one way or the other what he said, he seized the fame that lay to his hand. "I am one of the 'Borough Lot,'" he said, and was led out proud and handcuffed with the knowledge that he had established beyond dispute his title to consideration as a desperate criminal.

Mr. Spedding was a man who thought quickly. Ideas and plans came to him as dross and diamonds come to the man at the sorting table, and he had the faculty of selection. He saw the police system of England as only the police themselves saw it, and he had an open mind upon Angel's action. It was within the bounds of possibility that Angel had acted with full authority; it was equally possible that Angel was bluffing. Mr. Spedding had two courses before him, and they were both desperate; but he must be sure in how, so far, his immediate liberty depended upon the whim of a deputy-assistant-commissioner of police. Angel had mentioned a supreme authority. It was characteristic of Spedding that he should walk into a mine to see how far the fuse had burned. In other words, he hailed the first cab, and drove to the House of Commons. The Right Honorable George Chandler Middleborough, His Majesty's Secretary of State for Home Affairs, is a notoriously inaccessible man; but he makes exceptions, and such an exception he made in favour of Spedding. For eminent solicitors do not come down to the House at ten o'clock in the evening to gratify an idle curiosity, or to be shown over the House, or beg patronage and interest; and when a business card is marked "most urgent," and that card stands for a staple representative of an important profession, the request for an interview is not easily refused.

Spedding was shown into the minister's room, and the Home Secretary rose with a smile. He knew Mr. Spedding by sight, and had once dined in his company, "Er—" he began, looking at the card in his hand, "what can I do for you at this hour?" he smiled again

"I have called to see you in the matter of the late—er—Mr. Reale." He saw and watched the minister's face. Beyond looking a little puzzled, the Home Secretary made no sign.

"Good!" thought Spedding, and breathed with more freedom.

"I'm afraid—" said the minister.

He got no further, for Spedding was at once humility, apology, and embarrassment. What! had the Home Secretary not received his letter? A letter dealing with the estate of Reale? You can imagine the distress and vexation on Mr. Spedding's face as he spoke of the criminal carelessness of his clerk, his attitude of helplessness, his recognition of the absolute impossibility of discussing the matter until the Secretary had received the letter, and his withdrawal, leaving behind him a sympathetic minister of State who would have been pleased—would have been delighted, my dear sir, to have helped Mr. Spedding if he'd received the letter in time to consider its contents.

Mr. Spedding was an inventive genius, and it might have been in reference to him that the motherhood of invention was first identified with dire necessity.

Out again in the courtyard, Spedding found a cab that carried him to his club.

"Angel bluffed!" he reflected with an inward smile. "My friend, you are risking that nice appointment of yours." He smiled again, for it occurred to him that his risk was the greater. "Two millions!" he murmured. "It is worth it: I could do a great deal with two millions." He got down at his club, and tendered the cab-man the legal fare to a penny.

XI. — THE QUEST OF THE BOOK

WHEN Piccadilly Circus, a blaze of light, was thronged with the crowds that the theatres were discharging, a motor-car came gingerly through the traffic, passed down Regent Street, and swinging along Pall Mall, headed southward across Westminster Bridge. The rain had ceased, but underfoot the roads were sodden, and the car bespattered its occupants with black mud. The chauffeur at the wheel turned as the car ran smoothly along the tramway lines in the Old Kent Road and asked a question, and one of the two men in the back of the car consulted the other.

"We will go to Cramer's first," said the man. Old Kent Road was a fleeting vision of closed shops, of little knots of men emerging from public-houses at the potman's strident command; Lewisham High Road, as befits that very respectable thoroughfare, was decorously sleeping; Lea, where the hedges begin, was silent; and Chislehurst was a place of the dead. Near the common the car pulled up at a big house standing in black quietude, and the two occupants of the car descended and passed through the stiff gate, along the gravelled path, and came to a stop at the broad porch.

"I don't know what old Mauder will say," said Angel as he fumbled for the bell; "he's a methodical old chap." In the silence they could hear the thrill of the electric bell. They waited a few minutes, and rang again. Then they heard a window opened and a sleepy voice demand—

"Who is there?"

Angel stepped back from the porch and looked up. "Hullo, Mauder! I want you. I'm Angel."

"The devil!" said a surprised voice. "Wait a bit. I'll be down in a jiffy."

The pleasant-faced man who in dressing-gown and pajamas opened the door to them and conducted them to a cosy library was Mr. Ernest Mauder himself.

It is unnecessary to introduce that world-famous publisher to the reader, the more particularly in view of the storm of controversy that burst about his robust figure in regard to the recent publication of Count Lehoff''s embarrassing "Memoirs." He made a sign to the two men to be seated, nodding to Jimmy as to an old friend.

"I am awfully sorry to disturb you at this rotten hour," Angel commenced, and the other arrested his apology with a gesture.

"You detective people are so fond of springing surprises on us unintelligent outsiders," he said, with a twinkle in his eye, "that I am almost tempted to startle you."

"It takes a lot to startle me," said Angel complacently.

"You've brought it on your own head," warned the publisher, wagging a forefinger at the smiling Angel. "Now let me tell you why you have motored down from London on this miserable night on a fairly fruitless errand."

"Eh?" The smile left Angel's face.

"Ah, I thought that would startle you! You've come about a book?"

"Yes," said Jimmy wonderingly.

"A book published by our people nine years ago?"

"Yes," the wonderment deepening on the faces of the two men.

"The title," said the publisher impressively, "is A Short Study on the Origin of the Alphabet, and the author is a half-mad old don, who was subsequently turned out of Oxford for drunkenness."

"Mauder," said Jimmy, gazing at his host in bewilderment, "you've hit it—but—"

"Ah," said the publisher, triumphant, "I thought that was it. Well, your search is fruitless. We only printed five hundred copies; the book was a failure—the same ground was more effectively covered by better books. I found a dusty old copy a few years ago, and gave it to my secretary. So far as I know, that is the only copy in existence."

"But your secretary?" said Angel eagerly. "What is his name? Where does he live?"

"It's not a 'he,'" said Mauder, "but a 'she.'"

"Her name?"

"If you had asked that question earlier in the evening I could not have told you," said Mauder, obviously enjoying the mystery he had created, "but since then my memory has been refreshed. The girl—and a most charming lady too—was my secretary for two years. I do not know what induced her to work, but I rather think she supported an invalid father."

"What is her name?" asked Angel impatiently.

"Kathleen Kent," replied the publisher, "and her address is—"

"Kathleen Kent!" repeated Jimmy in wide-eyed astonishment. "Angels and Ministers of Grace defend us!"

"Kathleen Kent!" repeated Angel with a gasp. "Well, that takes the everlasting biscuit! But," he added quickly, "how did you come to know of our errand?"

"Well," drawled the elder man, wrapping his dressing-gown round him more snugly, "it was a guess to an extent. You see, Angel, when a man has been already awakened out of a sound sleep to answer mysterious inquiries about an out-of-date book—"

"What," cried Jimmy, jumping up, "somebody has already been here?"

"It is only natural," the publisher went on, "to connect his errand with that of the second midnight intruder."

"Who has been here? For Heaven's sake, don't be funny; this is a serious business."

"Nobody has been here," said Mauder, "but an hour ago a man called me up on the telephone—"

Jimmy looked at Angel, and Angel looked at Jimmy.

"Jimmy," said Angel penitently, "write me down as a fool. Telephone! Heavens, I didn't know you were connected."

"Nor was I till last week," said the publisher, "nor will I be after tomorrow. Sleep is too precious a gift to be dissipated—"

"Who was the man?" demanded Angel.

"I couldn't quite catch his name. He was very apologetic. I gathered that he was a newspaper man, and wanted particulars in connection with the death of the author."

Angel smiled. "The author's alive all right," he said grimly. "How did the voice sound—a little pompous, with a clearing of the throat before each sentence?"

The other nodded.

"Spedding!" said Angel, rising. "We haven't any time to lose, Jimmy."

Mander accompanied them into the hall.

"One question," said Jimmy, as he fastened the collar of his motor-coat. "Can you give us if any idea of the contents of the book?"

"I can't," was the reply. "I have a dim recollection that much of it was purely conventional, that there were some rough drawings, and the earlier forms of the alphabet were illustrated—the sort of thing you find in encyclopaedias or in the back pages of teachers' Bibles."

The two men took their seats in the car as it swung round and turned its bright head-lamps toward London.

"'I found this puzzle in a book From which some mighty truths were took,'" murmured Angel in his companion's ear, and Jimmy nodded. He was at that moment utterly oblivious and careless of the fortune that awaited them in the great safe at Lombard Street. His mind was filled with anxiety concerning the girl who unconsciously held the book which might tomorrow make her an heiress. Spedding had moved promptly, and he would be aided, he did not doubt, by Connor and the ruffians of the "Borough Lot." If the book was still in the girl's possession they would have it, and they would make their attempt at once. His mind was full of dark forebodings, and although the car bounded through the night at full speed, and the rain which had commenced to fall again cut his face, and the momentum of the powerful machine took his breath away, it went all too slowly for his mood.

One incident relieved the monotony of the journey. As the car flew round a corner in an exceptionally narrow lane it almost crashed into another car, which, driven at breakneck speed, was coming in the opposite direction. A fleeting exchange of curses between the chauffeurs, and the cars passed. By common consent, they had headed for Kathleen's home. Streatham was deserted.

As they turned the corner of the quiet road in which the girl lived, Angel stopped the car and alighted. He lifted one of the huge lamps from the socket and examined the road.

"There has been a car here less than half an hour ago," he said, pointing to the unmistakable track of wheels. They led to the door of the house. He rang the bell, and it was almost immediately answered by an elderly lady, who, wrapped in a loose dressing-gown, bade him enter.

"Nobody seems to be surprised to see us tonight," thought Angel with bitter humour.

"I am Detective Angel from Scotland Yard," he announced himself, and the elderly lady seemed unimpressed.

"Kathleen has gone," she informed him cheerfully.

Jimmy heard her with a sinking at his heart.

"Yes," said the old lady, "Mr. Spedding, the eminent solicitor, called for her an hour ago, and"—she grew confidential—"as I know you gentlemen are very much interested in the case, I may say that there is every hope that before tomorrow my niece will be in possession of her fortune."

Jimmy groaned. "Please, go on," said Angel.

"It came about over a book which Kathleen had given her some years ago, and which most assuredly would have been lost but for my carefulness."

Jimmy cursed her "carefulness" under his breath.

"When we moved here after the death of Kathleen's poor father I had a great number of things stored. There were amongst these an immense quantity of books, which Kathleen would have sold, but which I thought—"

"Where are these stored?" asked Angel quickly.

"At an old property of ours—the only property that my poor brother had remaining," she replied sadly, "and that because it was in too dilapidated a condition to attract buyers."

"Where, where?" Angel realized the rudeness of his impatience. "Forgive me, madam," he said, "but it is absolutely necessary that I should follow your niece at once."

"It is on the Tonbridge Road," she answered stiffly. "So far as I can remember, it is somewhere between Crawley and Tonbridge, but I am not sure. Kathleen knows the place well; that is why she has gone."

"Somewhere on the Tonbridge Road!" repeated Angel helplessly.

"We could follow the car's tracks," said Jimmy.

Angel shook his head. "If this rain is general, they will be obliterated," he replied.

They stood a minute, Jimmy biting the sodden finger of his glove, and Angel staring into vacancy.

Then Jimmy demanded unexpectedly—"Have you a Bible?"

The old lady allowed the astonishment she felt at the question to be apparent. "I have several."

"A teacher's Bible, with notes?" he asked.

She thought. "Yes, there is such an one in the house. Will you wait?"

She left the room.

"We should have told the girl about Spedding—we should have told her," said Angel in despair.

"It's no use crying over spilt milk," said Jimmy quietly. "The thing to do now is to frustrate Spedding and rescue the girl."

"Will he dare—?"

"He'll dare. Oh, yes, he'll dare," said Jimmy. "He's worse than you think, Angel."

"But he is already a ruined man."

"The more reason why he should go a step further. He's been on the verge of ruin for months, I've found that out. I made inquiries the other day, and discovered he's in a hole that the dome of St. Paul's wouldn't fill. He's a trustee or something of the sort for an association that has been pressing him for money. Spedding will dare anything "—he paused then—"but if he dares to harm that girl he's a dead man."

The old lady came in at that moment with the book, and Jimmy hastily turned over the pages. Near the end he came upon something that brought a gleam to his eye. He thrust his hand into his pocket and drew out a notebook. He did not wait to pull up a chair, but sank on his knees by the side of the table and wrote rapidly, comparing the text with the drawings in the book.

Angel, leaning over, followed the work breathlessly. "There—and there— and there!" cried Angel exultantly. "What fools we were, Jimmy, what fools we were."

Jimmy turned to the lady. "May I borrow this book?" he asked. "It will be returned. Thank you. Now, Angel," he looked at his watch and made a move for the door, "we have two hours. We will take the Tonbridge Road by daybreak."

Only one other person did they disturb on that eventful night, and that was a peppery old Colonel of Marines, who lived at Blackheath. There, before the hastily-attired old officer, as the dawn broke, Angel explained his mission, and writing with feverish haste, subscribed to the written statement by oath. Whereupon the Justice of the Peace issued a warrant for the arrest of Joseph James Spedding, Solicitor, on a charge of felony.

XII. — WHAT HAPPENED
AT FLAIRBY MILL

KATHLEEN very naturally regarded the lawyer in the light of a disinterested friend. There was no reason why she should not do so; and if there had been any act needed to kindle a kindly feeling for the distant legal adviser it was this last act of his, for no sooner, as he told her, had he discovered by the merest accident a clue to the hidden word, than he had rushed off post-haste to put her in possession of his information. He had naturally advised immediate action, and when she demurred at the lateness of the hour at which to begin a hunt for the book, he had hinted vaguely at difficulties which would beset her if she delayed.

She wanted to let Angel know, and Jimmy, but this the lawyer would not hear of, and she accounted for the insistence of his objection by the cautiousness of the legal mind. Then the excitement of the midnight adventure appealed to her—the swift run in the motor-car through the wild night, and the wonderful possibilities of the search at the end of the ride.

So she went, and her appetite for adventure was all but satisfied by a narrowly-averted collision with another car speeding in the opposite direction. She did not see the occupants of the other car, but she hoped they had had as great a fright as she. As a matter of fact, neither of the two men had given a second thought to their danger; one's mind was entirely and completely filled with her image, and the other was brooding on telephones.

She had no time to tire of the excitement of the night—the run across soaking heaths and through dead villages, where little cottages showed up for a moment in the glare of the head-lights, then faded into the darkness. Too soon she came to a familiar stretch of the road, and the car slowed down so that they might not pass the tiny grass lane that led to Flairby Mill. They came to it at last, and the car bumped cautiously over deep cart ruts, over loose stones, and through long drenched grasses till there loomed out of the night the squat outlines of Flairby Mill.

Once upon a time, before the coming of cheap machinery, Flairby Mill had been famous in the district, and the rumble of its big stones went on incessantly, night and day; but the wheel had long since broken, its wreck lay in the bed of the little stream that had so faithfully served it; its machinery was rust and scrap iron, and only the tiny dwelling-house that adjoined was of value. With little or no repair the homestead had remained watertight and weatherproof, and herein had Kathleen stored the odds and ends of her father's household. The saddles, shields, spears, and oddments he had collected in his travels, and the modest library that had consoled the embittered years of his passing, were all stored here. Valueless as the world assesses value, but in the eyes of the girl precious things associated with her dead father. The tears rose to her eyes as Spedding, taking the key from her hand, fitted it into the lock of a seventeenth-century door, but she wiped them away furtively.

Spedding utilized the acetylene lamp of the car to show him the way into the house.

"You must direct me, Miss Kent," he said, and Kathleen pointed the way. Up the oaken stairs, covered with dust, their footsteps resounding hollowly through the deserted homestead, the two passed. At the head of the stairs was a heavy door, and acting under the girl's instructions, the lawyer opened this. It was a big room, almost like a barn, with a timbered ceiling sloping downward. There were three shuttered windows, and another door at the farther end of the room that led to a smaller room.

"This was the miller's living room," she said sadly. She could just remember when a miller lived in the homestead, and when she had ridden up to the door of the mill accompanied by her father, and the miller, white and jovial, had lifted her down and taken her through a mysterious chamber where great stones turned laboriously and noisily, and the air was filled with a fine white dust.

Spedding placed the lamp on the table, and cast his eyes round the room in search of the books. They were not difficult to discover; they had been unpacked, and were ranged in three disorderly rows upon roughly constructed bookshelves. The lawyer turned the lamp so that the full volume of light should fall on the books. Then he went carefully over them, row by row, checking each copy methodically, and half muttering the name of each tome he handled. There were school books, works of travel, and now and again a heavily bound scientific treatise, for her father had made science a particular study.

The girl stood with one hand resting on the table, looking on, admiring the patience of the smooth, heavy man at his task, and, it must be confessed, inwardly wondering what necessity there was for this midnight visitation.

She had told the lawyer nothing about the red envelope, but instinctively felt that he knew all about it.

"Anabasis, Xenophon," he muttered; "Iosephus, Works and Life; Essays of Elia; Essays, Emerson; Essays, De Quincey. Wliat's this?"

He drew from between two bulky volumes a thin little book with a discoloured cover. He dusted it carefully, glanced at the title, opened it and read the title-page, then walked back to the table and seated himself, and started to read the book.

The girl did not know why, but there was something in his attitude at that moment that caused her a little uneasiness, and stirred within her a sense of danger. Perhaps it was that up till then he had shown her marked deference, had been almost obsequious. Now that the book had been found he disregarded her. He did not bring it to her or invite her attention, and she felt that she was "out of the picture," that the lawyer's interest in her affairs had stopped dead just as soon as the discovery was made. He turned the leaves over carefully, poring over the introduction, and her eyes wandered from the book to his face. She had never looked at him before with any critical interest. In the unfriendly light of the lamp she saw his imperfections—the brutal strength of his jaw, the unscrupulous thinness of the lip, the heavy eyelids, and the curious hairlessness of his face. She shivered a little, for she read too much in his face for her peace of mind. Unconscious of her scrutiny, for the book before him was all-engrossing, the lawyer went from page to page.

"Don't you think we had better be going?" Kathleen asked timidly.

Spedding looked up, and his stare was in keeping with his words.

"When I have finished we will go," he said brusquely, and went on reading.

Kathleen gave a little gasp of astonishment, for, with all her suspicions, she had not been prepared for such a complete and instant dropping of his mask of amiability. In a dim fashion she began to realize her danger, yet there could be no harm; outside was the chauffeur, he stood for something of established order. She made another attempt.

"I must insist, Mr. Spedding, upon your finishing your examination of that book elsewhere. I do not know whether you are aware that you are occupying the only chair in the room," she added indignantly.

"I am very well aware," said the lawyer calmly, without raising his eyes.

101

"Mr. Spedding!"

He looked up with an air of weariness. "May I ask you to remain quiet until I have finished," he said, with an emphasis that she could not mistake, "and lest you have any lingering doubt that my present research is rather on my own account than on yours, I might add that if you annoy me by whining or fuming, or by any such nonsensical tricks, I have that with me which will quiet you," and he resumed his reading.

Cold and white, the girl stood in silence, her heart beating wildly, her mind occupied with schemes of escape. After a while the lawyer looked up and tapped the book with his forefinger.

"Your precious secret is a secret no longer," he said with a hard laugh. Kathleen made no answer. "If I hadn't been a fool, I should have seen through it before," he added, then he looked at the girl in meditation. "I have two propositions before me," he said, "and I want your help."

"You will have no help from me, Mr. Spedding," she replied coldly.

"Tomorrow you will be asked to explain your extraordinary conduct."

He laughed. "Tomorrow, by whom? By Angel or the young swell-mobsman who's half in love with you?" He laughed again as he saw the colour rising to the girl's cheeks. "Ah! I've hit the mark, have I?"

She received his speech in contemptuous silence.

"Tomorrow I shall be away—well away, I trust, from the reach of either of the gentlemen you mention. I am not concerned with tomorrow as much as today." She remembered that they were within an hour of daybreak.

"Today is a most fateful day for me—and for you." He emphasized the last words. She preserved an icy silence.

"If I may put my case in a nutshell," he went on, with all his old-time suavity, "I may say that it is necessary for me to secure the money that is stored in that ridiculous safe." She checked an exclamation. "Ah! you understand? Let me be more explicit. When I say get the money, I mean get it for myself, every penny of it, and convert it to my private use. You can have no idea," he went on, "how comforting it is to be able to stand up and say in so many words the unspoken thoughts of a year, to tell some human being the most secret things that I have so far hidden here," he struck his chest. "I had thought when old Reale's commission was entrusted to me that I should find the legatees ordinary plain, everyday fools, who would have unfolded to me day by day the result of their investigations to my profit. I did not reckon very greatly on you, for women are naturally secretive and suspicious, but I did rely upon the two criminals. My experience of the criminal classes, a fairly extensive one, led me to believe that with these gentry I should have no difficulty." He pursed his lips. "I had calculated without my Jimmy," he said shortly. He saw the light in the girl's eye. "Yes," he went on, "Jimmy is no ordinary man, and Angel is a glaring instance of bad nomenclature. I nearly had Jimmy once. Did he tell you how he got the red envelope? I see he did not. Well, I nearly had him. I went to look for his body next morning, and found nothing. Later in the day I received a picture postcard from him, of a particularly flippant and vulgar character?" He stopped as if inviting comment.

"Your confessions have little interest for me," said the girl quietly. "I am now only anxious to be rid of your presence."

"I am coming to that," said the lawyer. "I was very rude to you a little while ago, but I was busily engaged, and besides I desired to give you an artistic introduction to the new condition. Now, so far from being rude, I wish to be very kind."

In spite of her outward calm, she trembled at the silky tone the lawyer had now adopted.

"My position is this," he said, "there is an enormous sum of money, which rightly is yours. The law and the inclination of your competitor—we will exclude Connor, who is not a factor—give you the money. It is unfortunate that I also, who have no earthly right, should desire this money, and we have narrowed down the ultimate issue to this: Shall it be Spedding or Kathleen Kent? I say Spedding, and circumstances support my claim, for I have you here, and, if you will pardon the suspicion of melodrama, very much in my power. If I am to take the two millions, your two millions, without interruption, it will depend entirely upon you."

Again he stopped to notice the effect of his words.

The girl made no response, but he could see the terror in her eyes.

"If I could have dispensed with your services, or if I had had the sense to guess the simple solution of this cursed puzzle, I could have done everything without embarrassing you in the slightest; but now it has come to this—I have got to silence you."

He put forward the proposition with the utmost coolness, and Kathleen felt her senses reel at all the words implied.

"I can silence you by killing you," he said simply, "or by marrying you. If I could think of some effective plan by which I might be sure of your absolute obliteration for two days, I would gladly adopt it; but you are a human woman, and that is too much to expect. Now, of the alternatives, which do you prefer?"

She shrank back against the shuttered window, her eyes on the man.

"You are doubtless thinking of the chauffeur," he said smoothly, "but you may leave him out of the reckoning. Had your ears been sharp, you would have heard the car going back half an hour ago—he is awaiting our return half a mile away. If I return alone he will doubtlessly be surprised, but he will know nothing. Do you not see a picture of him driving me away, and me, at his side, turning round and waving a smiling farewell to an imaginary woman who is invisible to the chauffeur? Picture his uneasiness vanishing with this touch. Two days afterwards he would be on the sea with me, ignorant of the murder, and curious things happen at sea. Come, Kathleen, is it to be marriage—?"

"Death!" she cried hoarsely, then, as his swift hand caught her by the throat, she screamed. His face looked down into hers, no muscle of it moved. Fixed, rigid, and full of his dreadful purpose, she saw the pupils of his pitiless eyes contract Then of a sudden he released hold of her, and she fell back against the wall. She heard his quick breathing, and closing her eyes, waited. Then slowly she looked up. She saw a revolver in his hand, and in a numb kind of way she realized that it was not pointed at her.

"Hands up!" She heard Spedding's harsh shout. "Hands up, both of you!"

Then she heard an insolent laugh. There were only two men in the world who would laugh like that in the very face of death, and they were both there, standing in the doorway, Angel with his motor goggles about his neck and Jimmy slowly peeling his gloves.

Then she looked at Spedding. The hand that held the revolver did not tremble, he was as self-possessed as he had been a. few minutes before.

"If either of you move I'll shoot the girl, by God!" said Spedding through his teeth.

They stood in the doorway, and Jimmy spoke. He did not raise his voice, but she heard the slumbering passion vibrating through his quiet sentences.

"Spedding, Spedding, my man, you're frightening that child; put your gun down and let us talk. Do you hear me? I am keeping myself in hand, Spedding, but if you harm that girl I'll be a devil to you. D'ye hear? If you hurt her, I'll take you with my bare hands and treat you Indian fashion, Spedding, my man, tie you down and stake you out, then burn you slowly. Yes, and, by the Lord, if any man interferes, even if it's Angel here, I'll swing for him. D'ye hear that?"

His breast heaved with the effort to hold himself, and Spedding, shuddering at the ferocity in the man's whole bearing, lowered his pistol.

"Let us talk," he said huskily.

"That's better," said Angel, "and let me talk first. I want you."

"Come and take me," he said.

"The risk is too great," said Angel frankly, "and besides, I can afford to wait."

"Well?" asked the lawyer defiantly, after a long pause. He kept the weapon in his hand pointed in the vicinity of the girl. Angel exchanged a word in an undertone with his companion, then—"You may go," he said, and stepped aside.

Spedding motioned him farther away. Then slowly edging his way to the door, he reached it. He paused for a moment as if about to speak, then quick as thought raised his revolver and fired twice. Angel felt the wind of the bullets as they passed his face, and sprang forward just as Jimmy's arm shot out. Crack, crack, crack! Three shots so rapid that their reports were almost simultaneous from Jimmy's automatic pistol sped after the lawyer, but too late, and the heavy door crashed to in Angel's face, and the snap of the lock told them they were prisoners.

Angel made a dart for a window, but it was shuttered and nailed and immovable. He looked at Jimmy, and burst into a ringing laugh. "Trapped, by Jove!" he said.

Jimmy was on his knees by the side of the girl. She had not fainted, but had suddenly realized her terrible danger, and the strain and weariness of the night adventure had brought her trembling to her knees. Very tenderly did Jimmy's arm support her. She felt the strength of the man, and, thrilled at his touch, her head sank on his shoulder and she felt at rest.

Angel was busily examining the windows, when a loud report outside the house arrested his attention. "What is that?" asked the girl faintly.

"It is either Mr. Spedding's well-timed suicide, which I fear is too much to expect," said Angel philosophically, "or else it is the same Mr. Spedding destroying the working parts of our car. I am afraid it is the latter."

He moved up and down the room, examined the smaller chamber at the other end, then sniffed uneasily.

"Miss Kent," he said earnestly, "are you well enough to tell me something?"

She started and flushed as she drew herself from Jimmy's arms, and stood up a little shakily. "Yes," she said, with a faint smile, "I think I am all right now."

"What is there under here?" asked Angel, pointing to the floor.

"An old workshop, a sort of storehouse," she replied in surprise.

"What is in it?" There was no mistaking the seriousness in Angel's voice. "Broken furniture? Mattresses?"

"Yes, I think there are, and paints and things. Why do you ask?"

"Jimmy," said Angel quickly, "do you smell anything?"

Jimmy sniffed. "Yes," he said quickly. "Quick, the windows!"

They made a rapid search of the room. In a corner Jimmy unearthed a rusty cavalry sabre.

"That's the thing," said Angel, and started to prise loose the solid shutter; but the wood was unyielding, and just as they had secured a purchase the blade snapped.

"There is an old axe in the cupboard," cried the girl, who apprehended the hidden danger.

With a yell of joy Angel dragged forth an antiquated battle-axe, and attacked the shutter afresh. With each blow the wood flew in big splinters, but fast as he worked something else was moving faster. Angel had not mistaken the smell of petrol, and now a thin vapour of smoke flowed into the room from underneath the door, and in tiny spirals through the interstices of the floorboards.

Angel stopped exhausted, and Jimmy picked up the axe and struck it true, then after one vigorous stroke a streak of daylight showed in the shutter. The room was now intolerably hot, and Angel took up the axe and hacked away at the oaken barrier to life.

"Shall we escape?" asked the girl quietly.

"Yes, I think so," said Jimmy steadily.

"I shall not regret tonight," she faltered.

"Nor I," said Jimmy in a low voice, "whatever the issue is. It is very good to love once in a lifetime, even if that once is on the brink of the grave."

Her lips quivered, and she tried to speak. Angel was hard at work on the window, and his back was toward them, and Jimmy bent and kissed the girl on the lips.

The window was down! Angel turned in a welter of perspiring triumph.

"Outside as quick as dammit!" he cried. Angel had found a rope in the smaller room in his earlier search, and this he slipped round the girl's waist.

"When you get down run clear of the smoke," he instructed her, and in a minute she found herself swinging in mid-air, in a cloud of rolling smoke that blinded and choked her. She felt the ground, and staying only to loose the rope, she ran outward and fell exhausted on a grassy bank. In a few minutes the two men were by her side. They stood in silence contemplating the conflagration, then Kathleen remembered.

"The book, the book!" she cried.

"It's inside my shirt," said the shameless Angel.

XIII. — CONNOR TAKES A HAND

IT is an axiom at Scotland Yard, "Beware of an audience." Enemies of our police system advance many and curious reasons for this bashfulness. In particular they place a sinister interpretation upon the desire of the police to carry out their work without fuss and without ostentation, for the police have an embarrassing system of midnight arrests. Unless you advertise the fact, or unless your case is of sufficient importance to merit notice in the evening newspapers, there is no reason why your disappearance from society should excite comment, or why the excuse, put forward for your absence from your accustomed haunts, that you have gone abroad should not be accepted without question.

Interviewing his wise chief, Angel received some excellent advice.

"If you've got to arrest him, do it quietly. If, as you suggest, he barricades himself in his house, or takes refuge in his patent vault, leave him alone. We want no fuss, and we want no newspaper sensations. If you can square up the Reale business without arresting him, by all means do so. We shall probably get him in—er—what do you call it, Angel?—oh, yes, 'the ordinary way of business.'"

"Very good, sir," said Angel, nothing loth to carry out the plan.

"From what I know of this class of man," the Assistant-Commissioner went on, fingering his grizzled moustache, "he will do nothing. He will go about his daily life as though nothing had happened; you will find him in his office this morning, and if you went to arrest him you'd be shot dead. No, if you take my advice you'll leave him severely alone for the present. He won't run away."

So Angel thanked his chief and departed. Throughout the morning he was obsessed by a desire to see the lawyer. By midday this had become so overmastering that he put on his hat and sauntered down to Lincoln's Inn Fields.

"Yes, Mr. Spedding was in," said a sober clerk, and—after consulting his employer—"Mr. Spedding would see him"

The lawyer was sitting behind a big desk covered with beribboned bundles of papers. He greeted Angel with a smile, and pointed to a chair on the other side of the desk.

"I've been in court most of the morning," he said blandly, "but I'm at liberty for half an hour. What can I do for you?"

Angel looked at him in undisguised admiration. "You're a wonderful chap," he said with a shake of his head.

"You're admiring me," said the lawyer, fingering a paperknife, "in very much the same way as an enthusiastic naturalist admires the markings of a horned viper."

"That is very nicely put," said Angel truthfully.

The lawyer had dropped his eyes on to the desk before him; then he looked up. "What is it to be?" he asked.

"A truce," said Angel.

"I thought you would say that," replied Spedding comfortably, "because I suppose you know—"

"Oh, yes," said Angel with nonchalant ease, "I know that the right hand which is so carelessly reposing on your knee holds a weapon of remarkable precision."

"You are well advised," said the lawyer, with a slight bow.

"Of course," said Angel, "there is a warrant in existence for your arrest."

"Of course," agreed Spedding politely.

"I got it as a precautionary measure," Angel went on in his most affable manner.

"Naturally," said the lawyer; "and now—"

"Oh, now," said Angel, "I wanted to give you formal notice that, on behalf of Miss Kent, we intend opening the safe tomorrow."

"I will be there," said the lawyer, and rang a bell.

"And," added Angel in a lower voice, "keep out of Jimmy's way."

Spedding's lips twitched, the only sign of nervousness he had shown during the interview, but he made no reply. As the clerk stood waiting at the open door, Spedding, with his most gracious smile, said—"Er—and did you get home safely this morning?"

109

"Quite, thank you," replied Angel, in no wise perturbed by the man's audacity.

"Did you find your country quarters—er—comfortable?"

"Perfectly," said Angel, rising to the occasion, "but the function was a failure."

"The function?" The lawyer bit at the bait Angel had thrown.

"Yes," said the detective, his hand on the door, "the house-warming, you know."

Angel chuckled to himself all the way back to the Embankment. His grim little jest pleased him so much that he must needs call in and tell his chief, and the chief's smile was very flattering.

"You're a bright boy," he said, "but when the day comes for you to arrest that lawyer gentleman, I trust you will, as a precautionary measure, purge your soul of all frivolities, and prepare yourself for a better world."

"If," said Angel, "I do not see the humorous side of being killed, I shall regard my life as badly ended."

"Get out," ordered the Commissioner, and Angel got.

He realized as the afternoon wore on that he was very tired, and snatched a couple of hours' sleep before keeping the appointment he had made with Jimmy earlier in the day. Whilst he was dressing Jimmy came in—Jimmy rather white, with a surgical bandage round his head, and carrying with him the pungent scent of iodoform.

"Hullo," said Angel in astonishment, "what on earth have you been doing?"

Jimmy cast an eye round the room in search of the most luxurious chair before replying.

"Ah," he said with a sigh of contentment as he seated himself, "that's better."

Angel pointed to the bandage. "When did this happen?"

"An hour or so ago," said Jimmy. "Spedding is a most active man."

Angel whistled. "Conventionally?" he asked.

"Artistically," responded Jimmy, nodding his bandaged head. "A runaway motor-car that followed my cab—beautifully done. The cab-horse was killed and the driver has a concussion, but I saw the wheeze and jumped."

"Got the chauffeur?" asked Angel anxiously.

"Yes; it was in the City. You know the City police? Well, they had him in three seconds. He tried to bolt, but that's a fool's game in the City."

"Was it Spedding's chauffeur?"

Jimmy smiled pityingly. "Of course not. That's where the art of the thing comes in."

Angel looked grave for a minute. "I think we ought to 'pull' our friend," he said.

"Meaning Spedding?"

"Yes."

"I don't agree with you," said Jimmy. "It would be ever so much more comfortable for you and me, but it will be ever so much better to finish up the Reale business first."

"Great minds!" murmured Angel, remembering his chief's advice. "I suppose Mr. Spedding will lay for me tonight."

"You can bet your life on that," said Jimmy cheerfully.

As he was speaking, a servant came into the room with a letter. When the man had gone, Angel opened and read it. His grin grew broader as he perused it.

"Listen!" he said. "It's from Miss Kent."

Jimmy was all attention.

"Dear Mr. Angel, Spedding has trapped me again. Whilst I was shopping this afternoon, two men came up to me and asked me to accompany them. They said they were police officers, and wanted me in connection with last night's affair. I was so worried that I went with them. They took me to a strange house in Kensington... For Heaven's sake, come to me!... "

Jimmy's face was so white that Angel thought he would faint.

"The hounds!" he cried. "Angel, we must—"

"You must sit down," said Angel, "or you'll be having a fit."

He examined the letter again. "It's beautifully done," he said. "Scrawled on a torn draper's bill in pencil, it might very easily be her writing."

He put the missive carefully in a drawer of his desk, and locked it.

"Unfortunately for the success of that scheme, Mr. Spedding, I have four men watching Miss Kent's house day and night, and being in telephonic communication, I happen to know that that young lady has not left her house all day." He looked at Jimmy, white and shaking. "Buck up, Jimmy," he said kindly. "Your bang on the head has upset you more than you think."

"But the letter?" asked Jimmy.

"A little fake," said Angel airily, "Mr. Spedding's little ballon d'essai, so foolishly simple that I think Spedding must be losing his nerve and balance. I'd like to bet that this house is being watched to see the effect of the note." (Angel would have won his bet.) "Now the only question is, what little program have they arranged for me this evening?"

Jimmy was thoughtful. "I don't know," he said slowly, "but I should think it would be wiser for you to keep indoors. You might make me up a bed in your sitting-room, and if there is any bother, we can share it."

"And whistle to keep my courage up?" sneered Angel. "I'll make you up a bed with all the pleasure in life; but I'm going out, Jimmy, and I'll take you with me, if you'll agree to come along and find a man who will replace that conspicuous white bandage by something less bloodcurdling."

They found a man in Devonshire Place who was a mutual friend of both. He was a specialist in unpronounceable diseases, a Knight Commander of St. Michael and St. George, a Fellow of the two Colleges, and the author of half a dozen works of medical science. Angel addressed him as "Bill"

The great surgeon deftly dressed the damaged head of Jimmy, and wisely asked no questions. He knew them both, and had been at Oxford with one, and he permitted himself to indulge in caustic comments on their mode of life and the possibilities of their end.

"If you didn't jaw so much," said Angel, "I'd employ you regularly; as it is, I am very doubtful if I shall ever bring you another case."

"For which," said Sir William Farran, as he clipped the loose ends of the dressing, "I am greatly obliged to you, Angel Esquire. You are the sort of patient I like to see about once a year—just about Christmas-time, when I am surfeited with charity toward mankind, when I need a healthy moral corrective to tone down the bright picture to its normal grayness—that's the time you're welcome, Angel."

"Fine!" said Angel ecstatically. "I'd like to see that sentence in a book, with illustrations."

The surgeon smiled good-humouredly. He put a final touch to the dressing.

"There you are," he said. "Thank you, Bill," said Jimmy. "You're getting fat."

"Thank you for nothing," said the surgeon indignantly.

Angel struck a more serious tone when he asked the surgeon in an undertone, just as they were taking their departure. "Where will you be tonight?"

The surgeon consulted a little engagement book. "I am dining at the 'Ritz' with some people at eight. We are going on to the Gaiety afterwards, and I shall be home by twelve. Why?"

"There's a gentleman," said Angel confidentially, "who will make a valiant attempt to kill one of us, or both of us tonight, and he might just fail; so it would be as well to know where you are, if you are wanted. Mind you," added Angel with a grin, "you might be wanted for him."

"You're a queer bird," said the surgeon, "and Jimmy's a queerer one. Well, off you go, you two fellows; you'll be getting my house a bad name."

Outside in the street the two ingrates continued their discussion on the corpulence that attends success in life. They walked leisurely to Piccadilly, and turned towards the circus. It is interesting to record the fact that for no apparent reason they struck off into side streets, made unexpected excursions into adjoining squares, took unnecessary short cuts through mews, and finally, finding themselves at the Oxford Street end of Charing Cross Road, they hailed a hansom, and drove eastward rapidly.

Angel shouted up some directions through the trap in the roof.

"I am moved to give the two gentlemen who are following me what in sporting parlance is called 'a run for their money,'" he said. He lifted the flap at the back of the cab, glanced through the little window, and groaned. Then he gave fresh directions to the cabman.

"Drive to the 'Troc,'" he called, and to Jimmy he added, "If we must die, let us die full of good food."

In the thronged grill-room of the brightly-lighted restaurant the two men found a table so placed that it commanded a view of the room. They took their seats, and whilst Jimmy ordered the dinner Angel watched the stream of people entering. He saw a dapper little man, with swarthy face and coal-black eyes, eyebrows and moustache, come through the glass doors. He stood for a breathing space at the door, his bright eyes flashing from face to face. Then he caught Angel's steady gaze, and his eyes rested a little longer on the pair. Then Angel beckoned him. He hesitated for a second, then walked slowly toward them. Jimmy pulled a chair from the table, and again he hesitated as if in doubt; then slowly he seated himself, glancing from one to the other suspiciously.

"Monsieur Callvet, ne c'est pas?" asked Angel.

"That is my name," the other answered in French.

"Permit me to introduce myself,"

"I know you," said the little man shortly. "You are a detective."

"It is my fortune," said Angel, ignoring the bitterness in the man's tone.

"You wish to speak to me?"

"Yes," replied Angel. "First, I would ask why you have been following us for the last hour?"

The man shrugged his shoulders. "Monsieur is mistaken."

Jimmy had been very quiet during the evening. Now he addressed the Frenchman. "Callvet," he said briefly, "do you know who I am?"

"Yes, you are also a detective."

Jimmy looked him straight in the eyes. "I am not a detective, Callvet, as you well know. I am"—he felt an unusual repugnance at using the next words—"I am Jimmy of Cairo. You know me?"

"I have heard of you," said the man doggedly.

"What you are—now—I do not know," said Jimmy contemptuously. "I have known you as all things—as an ornament of the young Egypt party, as a tout for Reale, as a trader in beastliness."

The conversation was in colloquial French, and Jimmy used a phrase which is calculated to raise the hair of the most brazen scoundrel. But this man shrugged his shoulders and rose to go. Jimmy caught his sleeve and detained him.

"Callvet," he said, "go back to Mr. Spedding, your employer, and tell him the job is too dangerous. Tell him that one of the men, at least, knows enough about you to send you to New Caledonia, or else—"

"Or else?" demanded the man defiantly.

"Or else," said Jimmy in his hesitating way, "I'll be sending word to the French Ambassador that 'Monsieur Plessey' is in London."

The face of the man turned a sickly green.

"Monsieur—je n'en vois pas la ncessit," he muttered.

"And who is Plessey?" asked Angel when the man had gone.

"A murderer greatly wanted by the French police," said Jimmy, "and Spedding has well chosen his instrument. Angel, there will be trouble before the evening is over."

They ate their dinner in silence, lingering over the coffee. The Frenchman had taken a table at the other side of the room. Once when Angel went out he made as though to leave, but seeing that Jimmy did not move, he changed his mind. Angel dawdled through the sweet, and took an unconscionable time over his coffee. Jimmy, fretting to be gone, groaned as his volatile companion ordered yet another liqueur.

"That's horribly insidious muck to drink," grumbled Jimmy.

"Inelegant, but true," said Angel. He was amused at the obvious efforts of the spy at the other table to kill time also. Then suddenly Angel rose, leaving his drink untasted, and reached for his hat.

"Come along," he said briskly.

"This is very sudden," remarked the impatient Jimmy.

They walked to the desk and paid their bill, and out of the corner of his eye Angel could see the dapper Frenchman following them out. They stepped out along Shaftesbury Avenue; then Jimmy stopped and fumbled in his pocket. In his search he turned round, facing the direction from which he had come. The dapper Frenchman was sauntering toward him, whilst behind him came two roughly-dressed men. Then Jimmy saw the two men quicken their pace. Passing one on each side of Callvet, each took an arm affectionately, and the three turned into Rupert Street, Angel and Jimmy following. Jimmy saw the three bunched together, and heard the click of the handcuffs. Then Angel whistled a passing cab. The captive's voice rose. "Stick a handkerchief in his mouth," said Angel, and one of the men obeyed. The two stood watching the cab till it turned the corner.

"There is no sense in taking unnecessary risks," said Angel cheerfully. "It is one thing being a fool, and another being a silly fool. Now we'll go along and see what else happens."

He explained as he proceeded: "I've wanted Callvet for quite a long time—he's on the list, so to speak. I lost sight of him a year ago. How Spedding got him is a mystery. If the truth be told, he's got a nodding acquaintance with half the crooks in London... had a big criminal practice before he went into the more lucrative side of the law."

A big crowd had gathered at the corner of the Haymarket, and with one accord they avoided it.

"Curiosity," Angel prattled on, "has been the undoing of many a poor soul. Keep away from crowds, Jimmy."

They walked on till they came to Angel's flat in Jermyn Street.

"Spedding will duplicate and triplicate his schemes for catching us tonight," said Jimmy.

"He will," agreed Angel, and opened the door of the house in which his rooms were. The narrow passageway, in which a light usually burned day and night, was in darkness.

"Oh, no," said Angel, stepping back into the street, "oh, indeed no!"

During their walk Jimmy had had a suspicion that they had been followed. This suspicion was confirmed when Angel whistled, and two men crossed the road and joined them.

"Lend me your lamp, Johnson," said Angel, and taking the bright little electric lamp in his hand, he entered the passage, followed by the others. They reached the foot of the stairs, then Angel reached back his hand without a word, and one of the two men placed therein a stick. Cautiously the party advanced up the stairway that led to Angel's room.

"Somebody has been here," said Angel, and pointed to a patch of mud on the carpet. The door was ajar, and Jimmy sent it open with a kick; then Angel put his arm cautiously into the room and turned on the light, and the party waited in the darkness for a movement. There was no sign, and they entered. It did not require any great ingenuity to see that the place had been visited. Half-opened drawers, their contents thrown on the floor, and all the evidence of a hurried search met their eyes. They passed from the little sitting-room to the bedroom, and here again the visitors had left traces of their investigations.

"Hullo!" Jimmy stopped and picked up a soft felt hat. He looked inside; the dull lining bore the name of an Egyptian hatter. "Connor's!" he said.

"Ah!" said Angel softly, "so Connor takes a hand, does he?"

One of the detectives who had followed them in grasped Angel's arm.

"Look, sir!" he whispered.

Half-hidden by the heavy hangings of the window, a man crouched in the shadow.

"Come out of that!" cried Angel.

Then something in the man's attitude arrested his speech. He slipped forward and pulled back the curtain.

"Connor!" he cried. Connor it was indeed, stone dead, with a bullet hole in the centre of his forehead.

XIV. — OPENING THE SAFE

THE four men stood in silence before the body. Jimmy bent and touched the hand. "Dead!" he said. Angel made no reply, but switched on every slight in the room. Then he passed his hands rapidly through the dead man's pockets; the things he found he passed to one of the other detectives, who laid them on the table.

"A chisel, a jemmy, a centre-bit, lamp, pistol," enumerated Angel. "It is not difficult to understand why Connor came here; but who killed him?"

He made a close inspection of the apartment. The windows were intact and fastened, there were no signs of a struggle. In the sitting-room there were muddy footmarks, which might have been made by Connor or his murderer. In the centre of the room was a small table. During Angel's frequent absences from his lodgings he was in the habit of locking his two rooms against his servants, who did their cleaning under his eye. In consequence, the polished surface of the little table was covered with a fine layer of dust, save in one place where there was a curious circular clearing about eight inches in diameter. Angel examined this with scrupulous care, gingerly pulling the table to where the light would fall on it with greater brilliance. The little circle from whence the dust had disappeared interested him more than anything else in the room. "You will see that this is not touched," he said to one of the men; and then to the other, "You had better go round to Vine Street and report this—stay, I will go myself."

As Jimmy and he stepped briskly in the direction of the historic police station, Angel expressed himself tersely. "Connor came on his own to burgle; he was surprised by a third party, who, thinking Connor was myself, shot him."

"That is how I read it," said Jimmy. "But why did Connor come?"

"I have been expecting Connor," said Angel quietly. "He was not the sort of man to be cowed by the fear of arrest. He had got it into his head that I had got the secret of the safe, and I he came to find out."

Inside the station the inspector on duty saluted him.

"We have one of your men inside," he said pleasantly, referring to the Frenchman; then, noticing the grave faces of the two, he added, "Is anything wrong, sir?"

Briefly enough the detective gave an account of what had happened in Jermyn Street. He added his instructions concerning the table, and left as I the inspector was summoning the divisional surgeon.

"I wonder where we could find Spedding?" asked Angel.

"I wonder where Spedding will find us?" added Jimmy grimly.

Angel looked round in surprise. "Losing your nerve?" he asked rudely.

"No," said the cool young man by his side slowly; "but somehow life seems more precious than it was a week ago."

"Fiddlesticks!" said. Angel. "You're in love."

"Perhaps I am," admitted Jimmy in a surprised tone, as if the idea had never occurred to him before. Angel looked at his watch.

"Ten o'clock," he said; "time for all good people to be in bed. Being myself of a vicious disposition, and, moreover, desirous of washing the taste of tragedy out of my mouth, I suggest we walk steadily to a place of refreshment."

"Angel," said Jimmy, "I cannot help thinking that you like to hear yourself talk."

"I love it," said Angel frankly.

In a little underground bar in Leicester Square they sat at a table listening to a little string band worry through the overture to Lohengrin. The crowded room suited their moods. Jimmy, in his preoccupation, found the noise, the babble of voices in many tongues, and the wail of the struggling orchestra, soothing after the exciting events of the past few hours. To Angel the human element in the crowd formed relaxation. The loud-speaking men with their flashy jewellery, the painted women with their automatic smiles, the sprinkling of keen-faced sharps he recognized, they formed part of the pageant of life—the life as Angel saw it. They sat sipping their wine until there came a man who, glancing carelessly round the room, made an imperceptible sign to Angel, and then, as if having satisfied himself that the man he was looking for was not present, left the room again. Angel and his companion followed.

"Well?" asked Angel.

"Spedding goes to the safe to-night," said the stranger.

"Good," said Angel.

"The guard at the safe is permanently withdrawn by Spedding's order."

"That I know," said Angel. "It was withdrawn the very night the 'Borough Lot' came. On whose behalf is Spedding acting?"

"On behalf of Connor, who I understand is one of the legatees."

Angel whistled. "Whew! Jimmy, this is to be the Grand Finale."

He appeared deep in thought for a moment.

"It will be necessary for Miss Kent to be present," he said after a while.

From a neighbouring district messenger office he got on by the telephone to a garage, and within half an hour they were ringing the bell at Kathleen's modest little house.

The girl rose to greet them as they entered. All sign of the last night's fatigue had vanished.

"Yes," she replied, "I have slept the greater part of the day."

Angel observed that she studiously kept her eyes from Jimmy, and that that worthy was preternaturally interested in a large seascape that hung over the fireplace.

"This is the last occasion we shall be troubling you at so late an hour," said Angel, "but I am afraid we shall want you with us tonight."

"I will do whatever you wish," she answered simply. "You have been, both of you, most kind."

She flashed a glance at Jimmy, and saw for the first time the surgical dressing on his head. "You—you are not hurt?" she cried in alarm, then checked herself.

"Not at all," said Jimmy loudly, "nothing, I assure you."

He was in an unusual panic, and wished he had not come.

"He tripped over a hearthrug and fell against a marble mantelpiece," lied Angel elaborately. "The marble has been in the possession of my family for centuries, and is now badly, and I fear irretrievably, damaged."

Jimmy smiled, and his smile was infectious. "A gross libel, Miss Kent," he said, recovering his nerve. "As a matter of fact—"

"As a matter of fact," interrupted Angel impressively, "Jimmy was walking in his sleep!"

"Be serious, Mr. Angel," implored the girl, who was now very concerned as she saw the extent of Jimmy's injury, and noticed the dark shadows under his eyes.

"Was it Spedding?"

"It was," said Angel promptly. "A little attempt which proved a failure."

Jimmy saw the concern in the girl's eyes, and, manlike, it cheered him.

"It is hardly worth talking about," he said hastily, "and I think we ought not to delay our departure a second."

"I will not keep you a moment longer than I can help," she said, and left the room to dress herself for the journey.

"Jimmy," said Angel, as soon as she had gone, "cross my hand with silver, pretty gentleman, and I will tell your fortune."

"Don't talk rot," replied Jimmy.

"I can see a bright future, a dark lady with big gray eyes, who—"

"For Heaven's sake, shut up!" growled Jimmy, very red; "she's coming."

They reached the Safe Deposit when the bells of the city were chiming the half-hour after eleven.

"Shall we go in?" asked Jimmy.

"Better not," advised Angel. "If Spedding knows we have a key it might spoil the whole show."

So the car slowly patrolled the narrow length of Lombard Street, an object of professional interest to the half-dozen plain-clothes policemen who were on duty there. They had three quarters of an hour to wait, for midnight had rung out from the belfries long before a big car came gliding into the thorough-fare from its western end. It stopped with a jerk before the Safe Deposit, and a top-hatted figure alighted. As he did so, Angel's car drew up behind, and the three got down.

Spedding, professionally attired in a frock-coat and silk hat, stood with one foot on the steps of the building and his hand upon the key he had fitted. He evinced no surprise when he saw Angel, and bowed slightly to the girl. Then he opened the door and stepped inside, and Angel and his party followed. He lit the vestibule, opened the inner door, and walked into the darkened hall. Again came the click of switches, and every light in the great hall blazed. The girl shivered a little as she looked up at the safe, dominating and sinister, a monument of ruin, a materialization of the dead regrets of a thousand bygone gamblers. Solitary, alone, aloof it rose, distinct from the magnificent building in which it stood—a granite mass set in fine gold. Old Reale had possessed a good eye for contrasts, and had truly foreseen how well would the surrounding beauty of the noble hall emphasize the grim reality of the ugly pedestal. Spedding closed the door behind them, and surveyed the party with a triumphant smile.

"I am afraid," he said in his smoothest tones, "you have come too late."

"I am afraid we have," agreed Angel, and the lawyer looked at him suspiciously.

"I wrote you a letter," he said. "Did you get it?"

"I have not been home since this afternoon," said Angel, and he heard the lawyer's little sigh of relief.

"I am sorry," Spedding went on, "that I have to disappoint you all; but as you know, by the terms of the will the fortunate person who discovers the word which opens the safe must notify me, claiming the right to apply the word on the combination lock."

"That is so," said Angel.

"I have received such a notification from one of the legatees—Mr. Connor," the lawyer went on, and drew from his pocket a paper, "and I have his written authority to open the safe on his behalf."

He handed the paper to Angel, who examined it and handed it back.

"It was signed today," was all that he said.

"At two o'clock this afternoon," said the lawyer. "I now—"

"Before you go any further, Mr. Spedding," said Angel, "I might remind you that there is a lady present, and that you have your hat on."

"A thousand pardons," said the lawyer with a sarcastic smile, and removed his hat. Angel reached out his hand for it, and mechanically the lawyer relinquished it. Angel looked at the crown. The nap was rubbed the wrong way, and was covered with fine dust.

"If you desire to valet me," said the lawyer, "I have no objection."

Angel made no reply, but placed the hat carefully on the mosaic floor of the hall.

"If," said the lawyer, "before I open the safe, there is any question you would like to ask, or any legitimate objection you would wish to raise, I shall be happy to consider it."

"I have nothing to say," said Angel.

"Or you?" addressing Jimmy.

"Nothing," was the laconic answer.

"Or Miss Kent perhaps—?"

Kathleen looked him straight in the face as she answered coldly—"I am prepared to abide by the action of my friends."

"There is nothing left for me to do," said the lawyer after the slightest pause, "but to carry out Mr. Connor's instructions."

He walked to the foot of the steel stairway and mounted. He stopped for breath halfway up. He was on a little landing, and facing him was the polished block of granite that marked where the ashes of old Reale reposed.

Pulvis Cinis et Nihil

said the inscription. "'Dust, cinders and nothing,'" muttered the lawyer, "an apt rebuke to one seeking the shadows of vanity."

They watched him climb till he reached the broad platform that fronted the safe door. Then they saw him pull a paper from his pocket and examine it. He looked at it carefully, then twisted the dials cautiously till one by one the desired letters came opposite the pointer. Then he twisted the huge handle of the safe. He twisted and pulled, but the steel door did not move. They saw him stoop and examine the dial again, and again he seized the handle with the same result. A dozen times he went through the same process, and a dozen times the unyielding door resisted his efforts. Then he came clattering down the steps, and almost reeled across the floor of the hall to the little group. His eyes burnt with an unearthly light, his face was pallid, and the perspiration lay thick upon his forehead.

"The word!" he gasped. "It's the wrong word."

Angel did not answer him.

"I have tested it a dozen times," cried the lawyer, almost beside himself, "and it has failed."

"Shall I try?" asked Angel.

"No, no!" the man hissed. "By Heaven, no! I will try again. One of the letters is wrong; there are two meanings to some of the symbols." He turned and remounted the stairs.

"The man is suffering," said Jimmy in an undertone.

"Let him suffer," said Angel, a hard look in his eyes. "He will suffer more before he atones for his villainy. Look, he's up again. Let the men in, Jimmy, he will find the word this time—and take Miss Kent away as soon as the trouble starts."

The girl saw the sudden mask of hardness that had come over Angel's face, saw him slip off his overcoat, and heard the creaking of boots in the hall outside. The pleasant, flippant man of the world was gone, and the remorseless police officer, inscrutable as doom, had taken his place. It was a new Angel she saw, and she drew closer to Jimmy. An exultant shout from the man at the safe made her raise her eyes. With a flutter at her heart, she saw the ponderous steel door swing slowly open. Then from the man came a cry that was like the snarl of some wild beast.

"Empty!" he roared. He stood stunned and dumb; then he flung himself into the great steel room, and they heard his voice reverberating hollowly. Again he came to the platform holding in his hand a white envelope. Blindly he blundered down the stairs again, and they could hear his heavy breathing.

"Empty!" His grating voice rose to a scream. "Nothing but this!" He held the envelope out, then tore it open. It contained only a few words—

"Received on behalf of Miss Kathleen Kent the contents of this safe."

"(Signed) JAMES CAVENDISH STANNARD, Bart.

CHRISTOPHER ANGEL."

Dazed and bewildered, the lawyer read the paper, then looked from one to the other.

"So it was you," he said. Angel nodded curtly.

"You!" said Spedding again. "Yes."

"You have robbed the safe—you—a police officer."

"Yes," said Angel, not removing his eyes from the man. He motioned to Jimmy, and Jimmy, with a whispered word to the girl, led her to the door. Behind him, as he returned to Angel's side, came six plain-clothes officers.

"So you think you've got me, do you?" breathed Spedding.

"I don't think," said Angel, "I know."

"If you know so much, do you know how near to death you are?"

"That also I know," said Angel's even voice. "I'm all the more certain of my danger since I have seen your hat."

The lawyer did not speak.

"I mean," Angel went on calmly, "since I saw the hat that you put down on a dusty table in my chambers—when you murdered Connor."

"Oh, you found him, did you—I wondered," said Spedding without emotion.

Then he heard a faint metallic click, and leapt back with his hand in his pocket. But Jimmy's pistol covered him. He paused irresolutely for one moment; then six men flung themselves upon him, and he went to the ground fighting.

Handcuffed, he rose, his nonchalant self, with the full measure of his failure apparent. He was once again the suave, smooth man of old. Indeed, he laughed as he faced Angel.

"A good end," he said. "You are a much smarter man than I thought you were. What is the charge?"

"Murder," said Angel.

"You will find a difficulty in proving it," Spedding answered coolly, "and as it is customary at this stage of the proceedings for the accused to make a conventional statement, I formally declare that I have not seen Connor for two days."

Closely guarded, he walked to the door. He passed Kathleen standing in the vestibule, and t she shrank on one side, which amused him. He clambered into the car that had brought him, followed by the policemen, and hummed a little tune. He leaned over to say a final word to Angel.

"You think I am indecently cheerful," he said, "but I feel as a man wearied with folly, who has the knowledge that before him lies the sound sleep that will bring forgetfulness." Then, as the car was moving off, he spoke again—"Of course I killed Connor—it was inevitable."

And then the car carried him away. Angel locked the door of the deposit, and handed the key to Kathleen. "I will ask Jimmy to take you home," he said. "What do you think of him?" said Jimmy.

"Spedding? Oh, he's acted as I thought he would. He represents the very worst type of criminal in the world; you cannot condemn, any more than you can explain, such men as that. They are in a class by themselves—Nature's perversities. There is a side to Spedding that is particularly pleasant."

He saw the two off, then walked slowly to the City Police Station. The inspector on duty nodded to him as he entered.

"We have put him in a special cell," he said. "Has he been well searched?"

"Yes, sir. The usual kit, and a revolver loaded in five chambers."

"Let me see it," said Angel. He took the pistol under the gaslight. One chamber contained an empty shell, and the barrel was foul. That will hang him without his confession, he thought.

"He asked for a pencil and paper," said the inspector, "but he surely does not expect bail."

Angel shook his head. "No, I should imagine he wants to write to me."

A door burst open, and a bareheaded jailer rushed in.

"There's something wrong in No. 4," he said, and Angel followed the inspector as he ran down the narrow corridor, studded with iron doors on either side.

The inspector took one glance through the spy-hole.

"Open the door!" he said quickly. With a jangle and rattle of bolts, the door was opened. Spedding lay on his back, with a faint smile on his lips; his eyes were closed, and Angel, thrusting his hand into the breast of the stricken man, felt no beat of the heart. "Run for a doctor!" said the inspector. "It's no use," said Angel quietly, "the man's dead." On the rough bed lay a piece of paper. It was addressed in the lawyer's bold hand to Angel Esquire. The detective picked it up and read it.

"Excellent Angel," the letter ran, "the time has come when I must prove for myself the vexed question of immortality. I would say that I bear you no ill will, nor your companion, nor the charming Miss Kent. I would have killed you all, or either, of course, but happily my intentions have not coincided with my opportunities. For some time past I have foreseen the possibility of my present act, and have worn on every suit one button, which, coloured to resemble its fellows, is in reality a skilfully moulded pellet of cyanide. Farewell."

Angel looked down at the dead man at his feet. The top cloth-covered button on the right breast had been torn away.

XV. — THE SOLUTION

IF you can understand that all the extraordinary events of the previous chapters occurred without the knowledge of Fleet Street, that eminent journalists went about their business day by day without being any the wiser, that eager news editors were diligently searching the files of the provincial press for news items, with the mystery of the safe at their very door, and that reporters all over London were wasting their time over wretched little motor-bus accidents and gas explosions, you will all the easier appreciate the journalistic explosion that followed the double inquest on Spedding and his victim.

It is outside the province of this story to instruct the reader in what is so much technical detail, but it may be said in passing that no less than twelve reporters, three sub-editors, two "crime experts," and one publisher were summarily and incontinently discharged from their various newspapers in connection with the "Safe Story." The Megaphone alone lost five men, but then the Megaphone invariably discharges more than any other paper, because it has got a reputation to sustain. Flaring contents bills, heavy black headlines, and column upon column of solid type, told the story of Reale's millions, and the villainous lawyer, and the remarkable verse, and the "Borough Lot". There were portraits of Angel and portraits of Jimmy and portraits of Kathleen (sketched in court and accordingly repulsive), and plans of the lawyer's house at Clapham and sketches of the Safe Deposit.

So for the three days that the coroner's inquiry lasted London, and Fleet Street more especially, revelled in the story of the old croupier's remarkable will and its tragic consequences. The Crown solicitors very tactfully skimmed over Jimmy's adventurous past, were brief in their examination of Kathleen; but Angel's interrogation lasted the greater part of five hours, for upon him devolved the task of telling the story in full.

It must be confessed that Angel's evidence was a remarkably successful effort to justify all that Scotland Yard had done. There were certain irregularities to be glossed over, topics to be avoided—why, for instance, official action was not taken when it was seen that Spedding contemplated a felony.

Most worthily did Angel hold the fort for officialdom that day, and when he vacated the box he left behind him the impression that Scotland Yard was all foreseeing, all wise, and had added yet another to its list of successful cases.

The newspaper excitement lasted exactly four days. On the fourth day, speaking at the Annual Congress of the British Association, Sir William Farran, that great physician, in the course of an illuminating address on "The first causes of disease," announced as his firm conviction that all the ills that flesh is heir to arise primarily from the wearing of boots, and the excitement that followed the appearance in Cheapside of a converted Lord Mayor with bare feet will long be remembered in the history of British journalism. It was enough, at any rate, to blot out the memory of the Reale case, for immediately following the vision of a stout and respected member of the Haberdasher Company in full robes and chain of office entering the Mansion House insufficiently clad there arose that memorable newspaper discussion "Boots and Crime," which threatened at one time to shake established society to its very foundations.

"Bill's a brick," wrote Angel to Jimmy. "I suggested to him that he might make a sensational statement about microbes, but he said that the Lancet had worked bugs to death, and offered the 'no boots' alternative."

It was a fortnight after the inquiry that Jimmy drove to Streatham to carry out his promise to explain to Kathleen the solution of the cryptogram. It was his last visit to her, that much he had decided. His rejection of her offer to equally share old Reale's fortune left but one course open to him, and that he elected to take.

She expected him, and he found her sitting before a cosy fire idly turning the leaves of a book. Jimmy stood for a moment in an embarrassed silence.

It was the first time he had been alone with her, save the night he drove with her to Streatham, and he was a little at a loss for an opening.

He began conventionally enough speaking about the weather, and not to be outdone in commonplace, she ordered tea.

"And now, Miss Kent," he said, "I have got to explain to you the solution of old Reale's cryptogram."

He took a sheet of paper from his pocket covered with hieroglyphics.

"Where old Reale got his idea of the cryptogram from was, of course, Egypt. He lived there long enough to be fairly well acquainted with the picture letters that abound in that country, and we were fools not to jump at the solution at first. I don't mean you," he added hastily. "I mean Angel and I and Connor, and all the people who were associated with him."

The girl was looking at the sheet, and smiled quietly at the faux pas.

"How he came into touch with the 'professor—!'"

"What has happened to that poor old man?" she asked.

"Angel has got him into some kind of institute," replied Jimmy. "He's a fairly common type of cranky old gentleman. 'A science potterer,' Angel calls him, and that is about the description. He's the sort of man that haunts the Admiralty with plans for unsinkable battleships, a 'minus genius'—that's Angel's description too—who, with an academic knowledge and a good memory, produced a reasonably clever little book, that five hundred other schoolmasters might just as easily have written. How the professor came into Reale's life we shall never know. Probably he came across the book and discovered the author, and trusting to his madness, made a confidant of him. Do you remember," Jimmy went on, "that you said the figures reminded you of the Bible? Well, you are right. Almost every teacher's Bible, I find, has a plate showing how the alphabet came into existence." He indicated with his finger as he spoke. "Here is the Egyptian hieroglyphic. Here is a 'hand' that means 'D,' and here is the queer little Hieratic wiggle that means the same thing, and you see how the Phoenician letter is very little different to the hieroglyphic, and the Greek 'delta' has become a triangle, and locally it has become the 'D' we know."

He sketched rapidly. "All this is horribly learned," he said, "and has got nothing to do with the solution. But old Reale went through the strange birds, beasts and things till he found six letters, S P R I N G, which were to form the word that would open the safe."

"It is very interesting," she said, a little bewildered.

"The night you were taken away," said Jimmy, "we found the word and cleared out the safe in case of accidents. It was a very risky proceeding on our part, because we had no authority from you to act on your behalf."

"You did right," she said. She felt it was a feeble rejoinder, but she could think of nothing better.

"And that is all," he ended abruptly, and looked at the clock.

"You must have some tea before you go," she said hurriedly. They heard the weird shriek of a motor-horn outside, and Jimmy smiled.

"That is Angel's newest discovery," he said, not knowing whether to bless or curse his energetic friend for spoiling the tte—tte.

"Oh!" said the girl, a little blankly he thought.

"Angel is always experimenting with new noises," said Jimmy, "and some fellow has introduced him to a motor-siren which is claimed to possess an almost human voice." The bell tinkled, and a few seconds after Angel was ushered into the room.

"I have only come for a few minutes," he said cheerfully. "I wanted to see Jimmy before he sailed, and as I have been called out of town unexpectedly—"

"Before he sails?" she repeated slowly. "Are you going away?"

"Oh, yes, he's going away," said Angel, avoiding Jimmy's scowling eyes. "I thought he would have told you."

"I—" began Jimmy.

"He's going into the French Congo to shoot elephants," Angel rattled on; "though what the poor elephants have done to him I have yet to discover."

"But this is sudden?" She was busy with the tea things, and had her back toward them, so Jimmy did not see her hand tremble.

"You're spilling the milk," said the interfering Angel. "Shall I help you?"

"No, thank you," she replied tartly.

"This tea is delicious," said Angel, unabashed, as he took his cup. He had come to perform a duty, and he was going through with it. "You won't get afternoon tea on the Sangar River, Jimmy. I know because I have been there, and I wouldn't go again, not even if they made me governor of the province."

"Why?" she asked, with a futile attempt to appear indifferent.

"Please take no notice of Angel, Miss Kent," implored Jimmy, and added malevolently, "Angel is a big game shot, you know, and he is anxious to impress you with the extent and dangers of his travels."

"That is so," agreed Angel contentedly, "but all the same, Miss Kent, I must stand by what I said in regard to the 'Frongo.' It's a deadly country, full of fever. I've known chaps to complain of a headache at four o'clock and be dead by ten, and Jimmy knows it too."

"You are very depressing today, Mr. Angel," said the girl. She felt unaccountably shaky, and tried to tell herself that it was because she had not recovered from the effects of her recent exciting experiences.

"I was with a party once on the Sangar River," Angel said, cocking a reflective eye at the ceiling. "We were looking for elephants, too, a terribly dangerous business. I've known a bull elephant charge a hunter and—"

"Angel!" stormed Jimmy, "will you be kind enough to reserve your reminiscences for another occasion?"

Angel rose and put down his teacup sadly. "Ah, well!" he sighed lugubriously, "after all, life is a burden, and one might as well die in the French Congo—a particularly lonely place to die in, I admit—as anywhere else. Goodbye, Jimmy!" He held out his hand mournfully.

"Don't be a goat!" entreated Jimmy. "I will let you know from time to time how I am; you can send your letters via Sierra Leone."

"The White Man's Grave!" murmured Angel audibly.

"And I'll let you know in plenty of time when I return."

"When!" said Angel significantly. He shook hands limply, and with the air of a man taking an eternal farewell. Then he left the room, and they could hear the eerie whine of his patent siren growing fainter and fainter.

"Confound that chap!" said Jimmy. "With his glum face and extravagant gloom he—"

"Why did you not tell me you were going?" she asked him quietly. She stood with a neat foot on the fender and her head a little bent.

"I had come to tell you," said Jimmy.

"Why are you going?"

Jimmy cleared his throat. "Because I need the change," he said almost brusquely.

"Are you tired—of your friends?" she asked, not lifting her eyes.

"I have so few friends," said Jimmy bitterly. "People here who are worth knowing know me."

"What do they know?" she asked, and looked at him.

"They know my life," he said doggedly, "from the day I was sent down from Oxford to the day I succeeded to my uncle's title and estates. They know I have been all over the world picking up strange acquaintances. They know I was one of the"—he hesitated for a word—"gang that robbed Rahbat Pasha's bank; that I held a big share in Reale's ventures—a share he robbed me of, but let that pass; that my life has been consistently employed in evading the law."

"For whose benefit?" she asked.

"God knows," he said wearily, "not for mine. I have never felt the need of money, my uncle saw to that. I should never have seen Reale again but for a desire to get justice. If you think I have robbed for gain, you are mistaken. I have robbed for the game's sake, for the excitement of it, for the constant fight of wits against men as keen as myself. Men like Angel made me a thief."

"And now—?" she asked.

"And now," he said, straightening himself up, "I am done with the old life. I am sick and sorry—and finished."

"And is this African trip part of your scheme of penitence?" she asked. "Or are you going away because you want to forget—" Her voice had sunk almost to a whisper, and her eyes were looking into the fire.

"What?" he asked huskily.

"To forget—me," she breathed.

"Yes, yes," he said, "that is what I want to forget."

"Why?" she said, not looking at him.

"Because—oh, because I love you too much, dear, to want to drag you down to my level. I love you more than I thought it possible to love a woman—so much, that I am happy to sacrifice the dearest wish of my heart, because I think I will serve you better by leaving you." He took her hand and held it between his two strong hands.

"Don't you think," she whispered, so that he had to bend closer to hear what she said, "don't you think I—I ought to be consulted?"

"You—you," he cried in wonderment, "would you—"

She looked at him with a smile, and her eyes were radiant with unspoken happiness. "I want you, Jimmy," she said. It was the first time she had called him by name. "I want you, dear."

His arms were about her, and her lips met his. They did not hear the tinkle of the bell, but they heard the knock at the door, and the girl slipped from his arms and was collecting the tea-things when Angel walked in. He looked at Jimmy inanely, fiddling with his watch chain, and he looked at the girl.

"Awfully sorry to intrude again," he said, "but I got a wire at the little post-office up the road telling me I needn't take the case at Newcastle, so I thought I'd come back and tell you, Jimmy, that I will take what I might call a 'cemetery drink' with you tonight."

"I am not going," said Jimmy, recovering his calm.

"Not—not going?" said the astonished Angel.

"No," said the girl, speaking over his shoulder, "I have persuaded him to stay."

"Ah, so I see!" said Angel, stooping to pick up two hairpins that lay on the hearthrug.

THE END

Printed in Great Britain
by Amazon